# Adventure

BRIAN DEASON

Copyright © 2016 Brian Deason

All rights reserved.

ISBN: 1523227141
ISBN-13: 978-1523227143

To Tara Perry

# CHAPTER 1

George Preston sat in his kitchen taking notes on *Sexuality in the Short Novels of Paul Manfred Harper*. He had recently started working on his dissertation, which would be about the quest for adventure, meaning, and fulfillment in an empty world in Harper's early fiction. George liked Harper's writing and found him fascinating as a person, but was repulsed by his machismo. Harper had lived from 1893 to 1972, the year of George's birth. Harper died in January; George was born in October. George was five feet, eight inches tall, and weighed a little over 160 pounds. He had red hair, freckles, wide shoulders, and a boyish face. He was wearing a dark green sweatshirt, old comfortable blue jeans that hadn't faded much, white boxer shorts, white socks, and white sneakers. He was a student at Southeastern Illinois University, in Sawyerville. It was a little after 3:00 p.m. on Thursday, January 20, 2000.

He heard a strange noise in the next apartment. It wasn't terribly loud, but it was puzzling, which made it more of a distraction to him. It was a kind of loud purr that came and then faded, like a powerful but efficient machine had somehow traveled through his neighbor's apartment. What would make such a sound? He frowned. He almost got up, but what was he going to do? Knock on his neighbor's door and ask what it was? He went back to work. Less than a minute later, he heard a similar sound.

He set down the pen, got up, and walked through a doorway into his living room/bedroom. He went to his bathroom, the door to which was closed. Beyond the bathroom was the next apartment. If he really wanted to know what it was he'd have to ask his neighbor. He was ready to do this now, even though he hardly knew her. But it was as if whatever it was was on the other side of the door in front of him. He looked at the doorknob. Knowing it was pointless, yet also knowing he wouldn't feel quite right unless he did it, he reached for the doorknob, turned it, and pulled open the door.

He was looking into a city street at night. From what he saw through the doorway, he was at street level, though his apartment here was on the third floor. There was a light rain falling in the city on the other side of the doorway. Immediately beyond the doorway was a sidewalk, then the street. He saw no vehicles and no people. He took a step so he was standing right in front of the doorway. He turned his head and saw his apartment—a television, his unmade bed, the window to the outside world in Sawyerville—the sun was out here. He looked back through the doorway. The rainy street was still there. Another vehicle went by. It made the sound he'd heard earlier, but louder. It looked a lot like a car but had no wheels—it sort of floated. The windows were black, while the rest of the vehicle was gray. He turned his head the other way and saw an armchair, the door to his closet, the door out of the apartment. Looking over his shoulder he could see through the doorway into the small kitchen; he could see some of his note cards, and a glass of iced tea he'd poured himself a few minutes ago.

He turned back to the rainy street. He was one step away from it. He thought about sticking his hand or even his head in, but didn't. He frowned, breathed in and blew out, puffing his cheeks a little. He breathed in again, hesitated, then stepped through the doorway. He felt the rain hitting him; it didn't feel bad. He let out his breath. He looked over his shoulder, and saw only a storefront. His world was gone. He was looking at a window display with mannequins wearing what looked like retro-1930s or '40s women's clothing. He nervously looked up and down the street. It was sinking in; he felt a little dizzy. He felt himself starting to panic. What had he done? He closed his eyes and sat down on the wet sidewalk. He tried to relax; he focused on breathing. The rain actually felt kind of good. He was here. He couldn't undo what he had just done, at least not right now. His life sucked anyway. He'd been thinking that this morning, and he thought it a lot. After a while, he got up.

Calmer, feeling a little better, he looked up and down the street again. He saw one vehicle, not the one he'd seen before but one a lot like it, driving away from him in the distance. There was some trash and a little broken glass here and there. There were street lamps with an old-fashioned look, but the lights were just glowing spheres. The buildings had a retro look as well, with lots of ornate trim, but they were much too tall to really look like '30s or '40s buildings. In fact they were considerably taller than what he was used to seeing in St. Louis. It made him almost dizzy again to look up at them. The whole thing, everything around him, had a kind of film noir feel to it.

He wasn't cold; the temperature was in the sixties. The street led to a T-intersection about half a block away to his left. He decided to walk that way.  As he approached the intersection he heard someone running.  Then he heard a splash like the person had run through a puddle.  He heard others running, and a screeching sound, and saw what seemed like a ball of light fly across the intersection.  He stopped.  A short man in dark clothing ran into the intersection, turned, and ran down George's street.  There was another screech and another ball of light.  The running man passed by him.  Then he saw two cops, also running, turn and come down his street.  What should he do?  He moved away from the line of fire, and then stood still.  He briefly considered running away himself, and decided that would be a very bad move.  This wasn't a movie.

The cops ran past him.  Their uniforms were dark blue but looked odd; it was like they were wearing leather armor.  One of them yelled, "Stop!"  The next moment the other shot at the fleeing man.  The ball of light hit the guy in the back, making a small explosion.  He fell to his knees, then—trying to turn, his momentum carrying him forward—onto his side.  Something that resembled lightning appeared, running from the wound up over and around his shoulder; it drifted, twisting and crackling, away from his body, and then disappeared.  With difficulty, the man got back to his feet and ran again, much slower now.  He was obviously finished.  The cops stopped running.  The one who had yelled stretched out his gun arm, sighted carefully, and fired.  The ball of light hit the man in the back with another small explosion.  He fell to his knees, then went down sideways.  There was more lightning, which drifted up and disappeared.  He rolled forward, face-down on the wet street, and didn't move again.

None of this looked good for George.  This was apparently the future, but an ugly future.  He didn't like his own chances with these cops.  The one who had fired the fatal shot was on the tall side, about six foot, slender, mid thirties, and had long blond hair he wore in a ponytail.  The other was short and squat, and looked powerful.  His skin looked very strange—it was horribly pitted and seemed to have a violet tinge.  Though one of them was tall and thin and the other was short and squat, they didn't seem at all comical.  They stood together and looked at him.  They didn't look at the man they had killed.  The short one put his gun in its holster; the other held his gun at his side.  The gun, George noticed now, was bulky, awkward-looking, and rather large.  He thought again about running.  Maybe he should have before, but now it was too late.  What was he doing here?  He looked at the fallen man.  More of the lightning crackled around him.  Through the big holes in his back, wires and metal were visible.  It was a robot.  George felt a little relief.

The cops came toward him.  The short one didn't look human.  This was a strange future.  George didn't say anything.  Neither did they.  They looked calm but unhappy.  As they got closer, the short one said, "Would you look at that get-up?"  The tall one didn't respond.  The remark had been made somewhat lightly, like the guy wanted to relieve the tension. But they both looked grave, the tall one especially.

They stopped in front of him. All three of them remained quiet a few seconds. George looked into the face of the short one, clearly not human, then the other. George said, "I'm a stranger here."

The short one, not unkindly: "Yeah. No kiddin'. So what's your pleasure, Sullok?"

Sullok curled his lip in distaste, and said, with a touch of sarcasm, "What's my pleasure?" He looked down, then up, then raised his gun so it was pointed at George's face. Sullok: "I'm sorry. It's not personal." Then George saw a flash of light, and heard a tremendous screech.

# CHAPTER 2

George heard a female voice: "Hendricks. He's coming around."

He opened his eyes. An attractive red-haired woman was looking down at him. He was lying on a bed. He was groggy, but trying to take it all in. The woman, who was standing next to the bed, looked familiar. A man approached the bed and also looked down at him. The man was balding but youthful. Now George knew who they were—Dirk Hendricks and J.P. Ryder, "Hendricks and Ryder" from *Hidden Agendas*. Which was absolutely insane.

Hendricks: "How do you feel, George?"

"Not too good." This couldn't be reality. He sat up. "Well, no, actually, I feel alright." He looked around. He was wearing the same clothes, still a little wet from the rain. He was apparently in a cheap motel room, sparse furnishings, walls painted beige. Through the window he could see a beautiful desert sunrise. "Where am I?"

Ryder: "You better lie down." He sighed, then did so. He felt emotionally numb. This was wrong. For some sort of window to open on a future world was wildly improbable but conceivable. But there could be no rational explanation for this. She continued: "We're in Second Chance, Arizona. Just outside of it, actually. We needed to get away from Los Angeles. And we needed to get you out of Pheonix. It wasn't safe." She was wearing a light blue suit, with pants rather than a skirt. Hendricks wore a dark blue suit and a maroon tie.

George: "Okay . . . . So . . . how do you know my name?"

She looked at Hendricks. He cleared his throat. "We could have gotten it off your driver's license. But to tell you the truth we've been looking for you for a while."

Ryder: "You knew that, didn't you?"

George: "Uh, no. I didn't know anything. I still don't." He sat up

5

again, and immediately swung his feet to the floor. Hendricks reached into his suit jacket and pulled out a gun. George: "What?"

Hendricks: "I just hope you're not planning on going anywhere."

George got up. "Just to that chair." He crossed the room to get to its only chair—old but comfortable-looking—and sat down. It wasn't as comfortable as it looked. He thought, then added, "I'm not worried about getting shot, anyway."

Hendricks sat on the bed and put the gun back in its shoulder holster. Ryder sat beside him. He asked, "And why is that?" His expression hadn't changed since George had arrived. Nor, for that matter, had hers.

George thought about Hendricks's question. "I'd rather not get into that. So what now?"

Hendricks and Ryder exchanged a look. Ryder sighed. After a long pause she said, "That kind of depends on you."

George waited for her to continue. She didn't. Eventually, he said: "Look, I think I'm a few pages behind. Maybe you better fill me in."

Ryder, after a pause: "Why don't you tell us what you remember?"

George thought about it. He definitely wasn't going to tell them what he really remembered. And that left him empty-handed. "I don't remember anything about you or this place or any conspiracy."

Neither of them responded. Then Hendricks said, slowly, "Conspiracy, George?"

He shouldn't have used the word. "Yeah."

Hendricks: "What do you know about a conspiracy?"

"I . . . I don't know anything you don't know."

Ryder: "And how do you know what we know?"

George, exasperated: "I watch the show." Actually, he'd only seen a few episodes all the way through.

They exchanged another look. Ryder, slowly: "Show, George? What show is that?"

George stood up and started for the door. "Jesus. Get me out of here."

There was a gunshot—the window shattered. They all hit the floor. There were several more shots. George looked over to the other two, who had their guns out. Hendricks, to George: "Don't do anything. Don't move. We'll handle this." More shots. Hendricks and Ryder crawled to the window, always staying beneath it. George had an impulse to stand and take a bullet, but he didn't. Hendricks rose and fired three shots in quick succession, then got back down. Whoever it was fired back. George rose a little and looked out—there was a large black car with two men and a woman behind it, all with handguns, all wearing suits.

Ryder: "Get down!" George did so. Why hadn't their enemies brought rifles, or other weapons more powerful than handguns? He knew the reason—because it was television. Ryder got up and fired twice, then got back down. She asked Hendricks, "What do you think?"

"I think it's time to leave. Okay with you, George?"

George shrugged. "Sure."

The door was next to the window; Hendricks reached up and unlocked it. The chain was still on, however. He fired a few more shots. The bad guys fired back. He and Ryder reloaded. He said: "We didn't find a gun on you. Don't ask me why." Sporadic fire continued to come through the window. Hendricks: "Okay, get ready. On three." He and Ryder got into crouching positions, ready to spring. George did the same. He felt a shot graze his back. "One . . . two . . . *three!*" They leapt up. Hendricks got the chain off in one smooth motion. The enemy shots intensified. Hendricks pulled the door open and the three of them burst out of the room.

Hendricks and Ryder fired steadily; so did their enemies. George saw the woman behind the car go down. He ran behind his two allies—they were all racing toward a medium-sized, average-looking blue car. They were on a gravel lot, and the only other car was that of their enemies. George's back hurt a little. He had an impression of spaciousness—there was nothing in front of them but their enemies, the blue car, and the desert. Hendricks reached the car first, a key ready in his hand. He got the driver's door open—he was no longer firing, maybe out of bullets—then quickly opened a back door. Their enemies kept firing, managing to miss at relatively close range despite their professional appearance. Ryder got off a last shot and then dove onto the back seat. Hendricks was already in the driver's seat, his door closed, starting the car. George dove in, landing painfully on Ryder, as the car sprang into motion, back door still open. Bullets hit the car as George reached back and pulled the door closed. A bullet hit the windshield and caused it to spiderweb. They were moving fast, kicking up gravel and a great cloud of dust. Ryder reloaded again. Hendricks: "Here, George." He tossed back his gun, which George tried but failed to catch. Then Hendricks tossed back a box of bullets, which George did catch. Now the black car was after them. They were on a narrow desert highway. George picked up the gun and started reloading himself. Hendricks: "We're trusting you."

"Thanks." There was occasional fire from their enemies. George finished reloading. Then he rolled down his window. He breathed in and out, and then stuck his head and arm out of the window and fired at the black car, trying to hit the driver. He missed the car. He felt wind blasting the back of his head. Their enemies continued to fire, occasionally hitting the blue car. He kept firing, hitting the other car once. Then Ryder put her head and arm out of her window and started firing. A bullet hit the other car's windshield, damaging it so severely that George could no longer see through it. The other car slowed down, then angled off the road. George and Ryder got back inside. He looked back. The other car stopped. All three of their enemies got out. There was blood on the woman's shoulder. She fired at the car one last time; the men didn't bother.

Ryder: "Nice shooting." She took the gun out of his hand before he realized what she was doing. But he didn't mind, anyway.

He wasn't sure who had hit the windshield. He assumed it was her, but it didn't really matter. Why did one shot do so much damage? He knew. He said, "Thanks."

Hendricks had slowed down a little but was still driving fast. "Listen, George, now that we seem to be on the same side, maybe you can tell us what's going on."

"I don't think so. I don't remember anything." This was more or less true, within the context of this world. Obviously, he was some sort of pre-existing character, who had had a role in the proceedings before he opened his eyes in the motel room. This was unlike the previous situation, in which he, apparently, walked into a story that had nothing to do with him.

Ryder: "You've got to remember something."

George: "I remember my name is George Thomas Preston. And I remember I'm from Unionville, Illinois, and I'm a grad student at Southeastern Illinois University. That's not much of a help, is it?" He'd grown up in Unionville, a suburb of St. Louis.

Hendricks: "Not too much."

George: "Look, I just had a gun in my hand and didn't try anything. Maybe you could tell me a little of what's going on."

Hendricks looked over his shoulder at Ryder, and nodded. "He's got a point."

Ryder: "You've heard of the Bureau of United States Affairs?"

George: "I know, you used to be agents. Now you're looking into various things on your own, including a vast government conspiracy."

Hendricks: "I thought you didn't remember anything."

George: "Well, I remember that much. It's pretty basic. Also, you're financed by various anti-conspiracy groups, especially the Seekers. Their slogan, and your slogan too, sort of, is 'Seek the truth.' And the conspiracy has covered up evidence of alien landings at Murphysboro and some other places." He knew all this just from casual viewing of the show, and hearing people talk about it.

Ryder: "So you know for a fact that's all true?"

George: "Oh yeah. But what about me? I don't know anything about myself."

Ryder: "Do you know anything about a BUSA official who always wears a gray suit and chews gum?"

George: "Gum-chewing Man. Of course." George got a kick out of

Gum-chewing Man, whom he had seen in two episodes. His gum chewing somehow made him seem more sinister.

Ryder: "Well, you and he were extremely close."

Hendricks: "I heard you were like a son to him."

That was an ugly thought. "To *him*?"

Ryder: "You did a lot of dirty work for the conspiracy. A lot of killing. We know of five examples. It's probably many times that." George didn't say anything. "Does that bother you?"

"Yes." He was more or less lying. It didn't bother him much, because he didn't believe any of this. He looked out the window. He liked the desert scenery. "Go on."

Ryder didn't say anything for a few seconds, then: "Do you remember those murders?"

"No."

Again she was silent a while; finally she said: "We found out a few days ago that the conspiracy had lost contact with you. They were trying to bring you in. One of them thought *we* knew where you were."

Hendricks: "We think they got to you. And that that's why you've lost your memory. Yesterday I got a tip about where I could find you. We drove to Phoenix and found you asleep on a park bench, drugged, just as my contact had said."

"So who's your contact? And why didn't they just kill me? By the way, is there any chance you could slow down?" They were going 70 on a two-lane highway in mediocre condition.

Hendricks gave a short laugh. "About the first question, I can't tell you that. . . . Second question, I don't know. . . . Third question, no, because we're in a hurry."

George: "And where are we going?"

Hendricks: "To meet a woman you know, Amy Mars, in San Diego. She's expecting us. Does the name ring a bell?"

"No. Why are we seeing her?"

"My contact recommended it. She might be able to fill us in on a few details. She might know more about you than you do."

George asked more questions, but learned little that he didn't already know. He didn't like that he was supposed to be such a sinister character here. They asked him more questions, but he had nothing to give them if he didn't tell them what he really remembered. He considered doing so, but decided not to. They wouldn't believe him, and he felt oddly reluctant to spoil this by hitting them with something so jarringly incongruent.

As attractive as the scenery was, it grew repetitious. Hendricks and Ryder didn't make small talk, and he would have felt strange doing so himself. How would they respond if he said something about the St. Louis Mavericks? Probably not well.

What was happening? Time travel wasn't out of the realm of possibility. Or maybe it was, but he was willing to assume it wasn't. But travel to a fictional world was not possible; or at least, he didn't see how it could be possible. The universe was a strange and mysterious place. He was sure there was much that, if he knew it and could understand it, would blow his or anyone else's mind. He would've accepted that before stepping into the rainy city, and he certainly accepted it now. But how could a person travel to a TV show? That just seemed totally beyond any kind of reality. Reality had broken down. Was there some sort of sentient agency running this? Maybe. That seemed like a good bet. Why were they doing it—what was the point? Why him? Would he find out? Enough; he didn't know where else to go with this. Eventually he decided to go to sleep. He figured he would probably wake up in a different world, or story, or whatever, but he didn't really mind.

When he woke up, he woke up slowly, not sure where he was at first. He realized he was in a moving car, then saw Hendricks and Ryder in the front seat and remembered everything. He felt another wave of panic, but again fought it down. He was surprised to still be here, but not really surprised he wasn't back in Sawyerville. At no point since all of this started had he thought he might be dreaming. Neither the rainy city nor this world was anything like his dreams—both seemed as real and as detailed as the world he knew, except that his being in them made no sense.

They were on an anonymous-looking four-lane highway surrounded by suburban terrain; there was quite a bit of traffic, and Hendricks was driving at a reasonable speed. It was a pleasant, sunny day.

Ryder looked back and noticed he was awake. "How you doing?"

"Fine. What day is it?"

She was surprised by the question. "Friday."

"I mean what day of the month?"

"The twenty-third."

"Of . . . what month?"

Pause. "March."

"Okay." He had to ask: "The year?"

Hendricks, after a longer pause: "1997. They did a good job on you George." He took an exit. "Maybe you'll get a chance to pay them back."

"Maybe."

Hendricks pulled into a gas station and drove up to a pay phone. Reaching through the open window, he picked up the receiver, put coins in, dialed, and quickly had someone on the other end. "Amy Mars? . . . This is Dirk Hendricks. Do you know who I am? . . . Good. We need to meet. Did you have a place in mind? . . . I don't know. How about something more public? . . . Perfect. Be on the first floor. We'll meet you there." He hung up and drove off. "We're meeting her at the Philtner Art Museum."

Ryder: "Anything coming back to you, George?"

"Nothing."

None of them said anything else on the way. They got back on the highway and stayed on it about 15 more minutes, the terrain soon shifting from suburb to city. George noticed how good their hair looked. Hendricks was losing his hair, but what he had looked very good. It occurred to George that their hair had looked perfect since he'd arrived. Maybe Ryder's had been affected a little when she stuck her head out of the window to shoot—he couldn't remember. But if so it wasn't much, and her hair looked perfect again now. This was what he would've expected, of course, but it was strange seeing it close-up, in real time. Hendricks took an exit that led them to a crowded street, drove a few minutes more, then turned onto the museum parking lot. He quickly found a spot close to the front entrance, and they got out of the car and went inside.

The Philtner Art Museum was spacious and looked great. As they entered through huge doors, George saw large abstract sculptures and large paintings tastefully arranged in an enormous room. Hendricks paid the admission for all of them. Suddenly George wondered how much money he had. Walking between the other two, he took out his wallet and checked. He had $17.60 (he kept change in a pocket in his wallet, unless it was more than a few coins). He also had his credit card, but it might or might not clear on this or some other world. He noticed that the wallet itself was pretty worn. He put it away. He was lucky he'd been wearing it when he entered the rainy city. It just as easily could have been sitting on his dresser.

Hendricks: "Amy?" They were approaching an attractive but disheveled and anxious-looking young woman in black jeans and a gray hooded sweatshirt. The woman nodded, then her eyes fixed on George. Her expression quickly changed. Her eyes blazed, she bared her teeth, and she rushed at him with an animalistic scream. Hendricks slipped behind her and grabbed her; he quickly had her in a full nelson.

She was still screaming. She yelled, "I'll kill you!" at George. He looked around. The rest of the museumgoers were looking at them. A tall black female guard was walking quickly toward them.

Hendricks whispered in Mars's ear, quietly but firmly: "Get a grip on yourself. You're letting them win. George is just an errand boy. If you keep your head we can get them all." This had an immediately effect—she stopped screaming, closed her eyes, took a breath, and relaxed.

The guard was in front of them; she had her hand on her gun. "What's the problem, folks?" Hendricks and Ryder were probably still wearing their guns. George hadn't seen them take them off, and now that he thought about it they hadn't passed through a metal detector. Nevertheless, he doubted anything would happen right now.

Mars said, "No problem." Hendricks let her go. She continued: "I just got a little upset, an anxiety attack. My friend was helping me out. Sorry we bothered you."

The guard nodded. "You're sure there's no problem, ma'am? I can help you if there is." She eyed the other three, one at a time.

Mars: "Oh, no. We're all friends."

The guard hesitated, suspicious. Finally: "Well, alright. Please call a guard if there's any problem. Have a good afternoon."

Mars: "You too." The guard left them.

Hendricks: "This isn't the best place to talk. Let's go outside." He led the way back to the front door, followed by Mars, then Ryder and George, walking side by side.

They went outside and then around the museum to a sculpture garden in the back. None of them spoke on the way. The garden was beautiful, with lots of bushes and flowers that complemented but didn't distract one from the sculptures. These varied from what looked like Grecian nude men and women to completely abstract, quite wild shapes and large, clunky formations of rusted metal. They found a pair of benches that faced each other and sat, Hendricks next to George and Ryder next to Mars. Mars and George sat diagonally to one another, which was as far apart as they could be and both be sitting on the benches. Ryder: "We don't have much time, Miss Mars. Why don't you tell us what you know?"

She gave a short, pained snort of laughter. Then: "Where do you want me to start?"

Ryder: "Start with George. What do you know about him?"

Mars: "I know he's one the most vicious, evil bastards on the face...."

Hendricks: "We already know that."

That was enough for George. He stood up. "I don't have to take that! This is all bullshit anyway!" He would have taken it if he had really done the terrible things his character had, but he hadn't. In fact he was beginning to seriously resent being put in such a role, though he didn't know who to be mad at.

Ryder, in a voice that was kind and exasperated at the same time: "George, wait." He did, against his better judgment.

Hendricks: "You need to just blow it off. We've got important work to do. And we don't have much time."

George: "Look, maybe I better just wait for you inside." Then he wondered why he should wait for them at all.

Hendricks: "No. That may be the last we see of you. Just please sit down. Please." His face showed a little expression, which impressed George.

Ryder, puzzled: "What do you mean, this is all bullshit?"

George: "Never mind. Let it go."

Mars: "What he did to me wasn't bullshit." Then her tone changed. "He also probably saved my life. It was like he was a different guy. . . ." Curious, George sat down again. Mars continued: "Okay. Here it is. I was a secretary with BUSA. I found some information I wasn't supposed to find. I didn't know what to do, so I disappeared. Well, I tried to. George found me. I should have known better than to trust him, but, as you know . . . ." She was silent a few seconds; when she resumed, her tone, briefly, was sarcastic: "He has a way with women. Anyway, he found me and brought me in. Not to BUSA, to the conspiracy. Of course I saw BUSA agents I knew. George told me they would torture me, and they did. He wasn't trying to scare me into talking; he just liked telling me." She gave him a hateful glare. "They wanted to know who I'd talked to. I told them the truth—I hadn't said anything to anyone. I wish I had. Of course, I didn't tell them *that*. Then I was in a cell for about a week." She was quiet again, and when she continued her tone was almost one of wonder: "Then George rescued me. It wasn't easy, either. He had to kill two men to do it. He got me out of there and he told me he was a new man. They wanted him to kill an eight-year-old boy, and they wouldn't take no for an answer. He said that's what turned him around. Anyway, he got me out of Washington, and we stayed together until Philadelphia. Then he gave me some money and said we needed to separate, and we did. Just like that. I came here. I figured I was safe, but I wasn't sure how to get the information out. Then yesterday a man called me at the motel I was staying at and told me he'd set up a meeting with you, and to stay where I was until you called. I have no idea who he was, or how he found me. Then today you called, and here I am."

Hendricks frowned, looked at Ryder, then back at Mars. He asked, softly, "What was the information?"

Mars: "The conspiracy. You know they've covered up evidence of alien landings?"

Hendricks: "Of course."

Mars, slowly: "The aliens are in on it."

Ryder, amazed: "What?" Even George was surprised. Then there was a sound like an air gun being fired; a small red hole appeared on Mars's forehead, and she slumped back. The other three were on their feet immediately, George and Hendricks turning, Hendricks and Ryder reaching for their guns.

A voice George had heard before said, "Stop or you'll die instantly."

Hendricks and Ryder complied. Hendricks sighed. "Why did you do it, Mr. Smith? Your predecessor had more finesse."

Then George realized who it was. Furious, he yelled, "Where are you, you son-of-a-bitch?"

Hendricks: "Take it easy."

The man called Sullok in the previous world stepped out of the bushes. He wore a black suit, black gloves, and a dark red tie. His hair was still in a ponytail. He had a gun in his hand, pointed at George. The gun had a silencer. "Exactly, George. Take it easy."

George: "Yeah, fuck you. You want to tell me what's going on, Sullok?"

Hendricks and Ryder: "Sullok?"

"What are you talking about? My name isn't Sullok."

George: "It's what you called yourself before, and we both know it."

Sullok, irritated: "Before what?"

"In that future world. On that city street."

Sullok looked mildly confused. Ryder: "Future world?"

George: "You shot that robot."

Hendricks: "What the hell . . . ?" George looked at him. He seemed very confused. Then he recovered: "They've messed with your memory, George."

George didn't even consider this. "Yeah, right. Look, could you stay out of this? It doesn't concern you."

Ryder: "Why'd you kill her, Mr. Smith? Or should I say Sullok?"

Sullok, firmly: "That's not my name."

George, getting annoyed, to Hendricks and Ryder: "Just, would the two of you drop the *Hidden Agendas* crap."

Hendricks: "Hidden agendas are why we came here. You know that."

George, shouting: "I came here because you brought me!"

Sullok, sadly: "If I told you all I know, you couldn't handle it."

George: "Yeah, I'll bet that's true." He looked around, then impulsively reached into Ryder's suit jacket, grabbed the gun in her shoulder holster, struggled briefly with her, and pulled out the gun. He quickly swung it to Sullok—who'd had ample time to shoot him—and fumbled with the safety, eventually getting it off. He yelled: "Go ahead and shoot! I don't care!"

Sullok: "Calm down."

George actually did calm down a little. With his tone controlled rather than angry, he said: "Yeah, Sullok, calm this down—you either tell me what's going on or I'm gonna blow you away. Right now."

Ryder: "George, that's not the answer."

George, angry again: "Would you shut up!"

Sullok: "Aren't you afraid of what will happen?"

George looked back at him, and raised the gun so it was pointed between his eyes. "I'll take my chances."

Sullok put his gun in its shoulder holster, under his jacket. "Alright. Go ahead." He raised his chin slightly.

"Done." George squeezed the trigger. He heard the shot, and saw a red wound appear between Sullok's eyes.

# CHAPTER 3

George was on a beach. He was surrounded by happy people, most apparently in their late teens or early twenties, and most in bikinis and swim trunks. They were engaged in various fun-in-the-sun activities. He saw a volleyball game, people running around, a couple building a sandcastle, and some people batting around a beach ball. Out on the ocean he saw a few people on jet skis, and a few others surfing. There were people coming out of the ocean, laughing particularly hard. Most of the people, male and female, were very attractive in a bland way, with fit bodies—lean in the case of the women, muscular but not too muscular in the case of the men—and conventionally appealing faces. It was a beautiful, sunny day, with lots of blue sky and a few puffy white clouds. He heard the song "Tidal Wave" played a little faster than usual. The temperature was in the eighties—it felt good. Many of the people around him were drinking cans and plastic bottles of Xerxi-Cola. He looked around and saw a band, four guys in swim trunks, playing enthusiastically, all concentrating but smiling. He said, "Curiouser and curiouser." He still had the gun in his hand. He put it in the waistband of his jeans, in front, and covered it with his sweatshirt.

A few people looked briefly in George's direction. A short woman with black hair stopped running to eye him for about a second, then resumed her run. They weren't treating him like he was invisible, but they weren't paying any special attention to him either. They were paying a lot of attention to their sodas. Apparently this was a Xerxi commercial. As if the *Hidden Agendas* world had not been absurd enough. He shook his head. Actually, he hadn't seen a Xerxi ad like this in years. The newer ads sought to identify the cola with the latest generation of teens. Whatever—he wasn't going to play along. He wanted to talk to Sullok. He looked around but didn't see the man, or whatever he was. He yelled, "Sullok!"

Quite a few of the nearby people looked at him, their smiles fading a bit. He said, "Screw this." He started walking along the beach, moving determinedly rather than strolling, looking for Sullok.

A blond man in blue trunks ran up to him and held out a can. In a friendly, happy way, he said, "Hey, lighten up, man!"

George kept walking. "Yeah, whatever." Then he stopped—he didn't like being rude to someone who was being friendly. He didn't consider this person real, but he still didn't want to be a jerk. He turned to face the happy man. "Thanks a lot, but I'll pass." He started walking again, and added, "Have fun."

The guy took this in stride. "Okay, man. I will." George looked over his shoulder—the guy was running back to the volleyball game.

George continued along the beach, yelling "Sullok!" and looking around. He was in a bad mood and was inclined to glare, but anytime he met someone's eyes, the person was smiling, and he felt obliged to smile back. After a few smiles he didn't feel like glaring anymore; he soon had a pleasant expression on his face. This gradually changed his mood. He moved toward cheerfulness, which bothered him a little. He had good reason to be angry.

A guy said, "Hey, dude!"

George: "Hi."

A woman, soon after: "What's up?"

George: "Hi. Not a lot."

A little boy: "Hey, mister!"

George: "Hey." His mood was better, but still dark by their standards. He wasn't getting into it all, and didn't want to, but he wouldn't be ruining it for them if it was real. He stopped yelling for Sullok after a while, but kept moving and kept looking for him.

A brown-haired woman wearing glasses approached him, laughing. She had a deep tan and wore an orange and blue striped bikini. "You need a Xerxi!" she said, and thrust a can at him enthusiastically.

"Hi."

"Would you like a Xerxi?" she asked, as if she was addressing a child.

"Uh, sure." He took it; it felt ice-cold in his hand.

"See ya!" she said, and ran off.

There were sexy women everywhere, many more per square foot, by far, than he'd ever seen on a real beach. But he considered them unreal. He wondered what he wanted. He knew he wanted to leave this place. Where did he want to go? Back home? That sounded dreary. To another of these worlds? There was an excellent chance the next one would be less appealing. The last one had been. He opened the can and drank. He'd been thirsty and hadn't realized it—the soda tasted good.

A guy yelled, "Hey, dude!"

George looked over.

"Yeah, you in the jeans! Want to play volleyball?"

He yelled back, "No thanks!"

"That's cool!"

Shortly after that, for no apparent reason, everyone on the beach except George yelled, "X marks the spot!"—Xerxi's slogan back when it used commercials like this. As they yelled, they all held up their drinks. Then they yelled, triumphantly, "Xerxi!"

A little while after that, a woman called to him to take off his sweatshirt. Just for the hell of it, he did so. He had only his skin underneath. The sweatshirt had been bothering him a little anyway in the heat.

The same woman yelled, "Nice gun!"

George had forgotten he was wearing it. "Thanks!" He decided to leave the sweatshirt off and let the gun show. What were they going to do—arrest him? He tied the sweatshirt around his waist, making no effort to hide the gun. People started looking at him, their smiling expressions slowly changing to looks of confusion. He put the sweatshirt back on, covering the gun. The looks of confusion went away.

He reached a place where the beach became rocky, beyond which there were few people. He said, "Screw it," not really angrily, regarding the whole beach scene, and walked inland.

Beyond the beach there was a picnic area, again with happy people drinking Xerxi. These people, however, were primarily in family groups. There were even a few elderly people, just as happy as everyone else, and of course drinking Xerxi. He nodded, smiled, and occasionally answered greetings as he walked through.

Past the picnic zone was a big parking lot. There was a variety of vehicles, mostly cars but also pickups, minivans, and jeeps. All of them were new. There were lots of bumper stickers, all related to Xerxi—he saw "Xerxi" in the particular Xerxi cursive lettering over and over. The few people here were happy, young, and drank the cola. George for some reason thought of something he'd heard in a class years ago. He said, "Beneath the pavement lies the beach."

He kept walking. Past the parking lot was a road; he followed it. There were lots of vehicles, most headed toward instead of away from the beach, all new, most with Xerxi bumper stickers. All of them had happy people in them; most of these were young and attractive, and most had Xerxis in their hands.

He was definitely sick of this now. Where was Sullok? Maybe he wouldn't see the man again, after all. And truthfully, while he would have liked to ask Sullok questions, so far the guy had done him little if any good. So now what should George do? On a whim, he pulled his gun out of his jeans and fired it straight up. The noise and recoil weren't that much but they made him flinch, anyway, as they hadn't in the previous world, when the shots had not been out of place. The people in the vehicles seemed momentarily stunned, then laughed and held their sodas up to George in salute. He waved the gun in response, then put it away.

He decided to try his luck hitchhiking. He stuck his thumb out, and the first vehicle—a big, red, sexy convertible with two young couples in it—stopped for him. The driver, a beautiful woman, asked, "Need a ride?"

"Yes. Thank you." He climbed into the back seat. The man next to him, who wore swim trunks and a button shirt that was completely unbuttoned, tapped George's Xerxi can with his own Xerxi bottle. "Cheers," said George. The vehicle started moving again.

"Yeah, cheers. So where ya headed?"

"I don't know exactly. Where you guys headed?"

They all laughed. The driver said: "I don't know. Around." They laughed again. A vacuous pop song came on the radio, and they all started to sing along with it. George ignored them, but kept his pleasant expression. He didn't really mind the song, anyway.

A young woman in the back seat leaned across the guy she was with and said to George, "Come on, what's the matter?" while the rest continued to sing.

"I just don't feel like singing. No big deal."

"Cool."

By the end of the song they were driving through a street lined on either side with pleasant shops. The street surface was red brick in a zigzag pattern, which was nevertheless smooth. It seemed to have been laid the day before. Among the shops were places selling clothing, ice cream, hot dogs, gyros, records, books, posters, surf boards, and scuba gear. People walked contentedly along both sides of the street. There was just the right number of people to make the area seem active but not crowded. It was wonderfully sunny. Many of the people wore swimsuits, many wore rollerblades or rode skateboards, most were under 25, most drank Xerxi, and all were happy. There was one shop with a large sign that read, simply, "Xerxi." George: "Could I get out here, please?"

The driver: "Sure!" She hit the brakes, not quite slamming them on.

The suddenness of it surprised George, but they weren't being rude. He climbed out. "Thanks a lot."

The driver: "No sweat." They waved and said goodbye, their manner suggesting he was a good friend, then drove away.

George walked into the Xerxi shop. Sullok was behind the counter. There were people around the counter, talking and laughing with him. He wore a blue and green striped uniform, with "Xerxi" across his shirt pocket. Again his hair was in a ponytail. The place was like an ice-cream shop, with quaint little round tables and little round-seated chairs with fragile-looking backs, but all they sold was Xerxi-Cola. The place was about two-thirds full, and the sun shone in nicely. The customers were of the same attractive sort George had seen outside; two of them wore rollerblades, and one preadolescent boy had a skateboard parked next to him at his table. A few of the males, like George, weren't wearing shirts. Everyone in the place had a Xerxi in his or her hand. This included George, since he was still holding the can.

He approached the counter. No one seemed to be waiting to be served; they were just hanging out with the cool counter guy. Sullok was smiling but not quite as much as the norm in this world, and unlike the vast majority of the people here he did not have a vacuous look. He said to George, pleasantly, "Hi, can I help ya out?"

George, aggressively: "Oh, yeah." Then he stopped. How should he play this? If he simply asked direct questions about what was going on, Sullok would play dumb. Yet he suspected there was some way he could get information out of the man.

Sullok, as pleasant as before: "What can I get ya?"

George smiled, amused by the question. "What do you have?"

"We got Xerxi. Bottles, cans, fountain, any size, whatever ya need. We've got glass bottles, if ya need one."

George's can of Xerxi was a little less than half full. But he wanted to order something, to keep the conversation going. He saw an old-fashioned eight-ounce glass bottle on a display shelf behind Sullok. "How 'bout one of those little bottles?"

"You got it!" Sullok reached under the counter and pulled out such a bottle, with the distinct Xerxi swirling design, wet and with little bits of ice sticking to it, looking very inviting. He placed it on the counter. "Twenty-five cents."

George set down the can, took out his wallet, took out a quarter, and tossed it to Sullok, who caught it, overhand. Then George picked up the bottle. He grabbed the cap to twist it off, then remembered you couldn't do that with these bottles. He looked at the counter—there was an old-fashioned bottle opener. He used it and then took a drink; it was delicious. He'd always liked the taste of Xerxi. He picked the can back up, perversely wanting to have a Xerxi in each hand so he would look odd. "So what are you guys talking about?"

Everyone but George laughed. Sullok: "Oh, this and that. Surfing. Skating. Volleyball. *Girls*." They laughed again.

George: "So, you like it here?"

"What's not to like?" Laughter.

Another tall guy, a teenager, asked George: "How 'bout you? *You* like it here?"

George, after another swig from his bottle: "Uh, I don't know. It's okay." He eyed Sullok. "You wouldn't believe where I just was."

"Try me."

"It's a long story."

Sullok raised his arms in a big shrug. "I'm a long guy." Laughter.

"Ever watch *Hidden Agendas*?" George thought they were probably still making commercials like this when the show began.

Sullok, frowning: "I've seen it."

"Well that's where I was."

The teenaged guy: "No way, man. You met Sara Faulkner." She was the actress who played Ryder.

George: "Yes and no."

Sullok seemed to be weighing his options. "So," he said, and paused. "Did you like it there?"

"Uh . . . no. Not my thing."

"So where would you like to be?"

"I have a choice?"

"Yes and no."

George thought quickly. "A Pistol Kramer adventure."

"Comin' right up." Sullok opened a glass cabinet-door behind him, took out a glass mug with "Xerxi" etched on it in Xerxi script, swung to a soda fountain, hit a lever to put ice in the glass, then hit another to put liquid in the glass. The liquid seemed like Xerxi on its way into the glass, but in the glass it looked strange. Once the glass was full, Sullok set it smartly on the counter in front of George. "On the house."

George hesitated. Mixed in with the ice were swirling images. He set down the can and the bottle and picked up the glass so he could look at it more closely. The images swirled into one another, but they seemed to be from the Pistol Kramer movies. He sniffed the liquid—it had no smell. He asked, "Whose house?"

"The house."

"Okay. See ya." He took a sip, and was sucked into the liquid.

# CHAPTER 4

George was standing in a jungle. A man was in front of him, walking; George followed. It was hot and humid. Birds and insects created a din with which George was familiar through old movies, but it was much louder being inside of it. The foliage was dense. The man hacked his way through it with a machete. They were moving upward. The guy was of medium build and wore khakis, cowboy boots, a gun in a cowboy holster, a white long-sleeved shirt, a loose-fitting gray vest, a gray backpack, a red handkerchief tied around his neck, and a gray fedora. It was Pistol Kramer. Under the hat, George knew, Kramer was completely bald.

He was the sidekick, but that was okay. He had asked for this adventure—he planned to play ball. He had seen all four Pistol Kramer movies. All were set around 1900, give or take a few years. This didn't look like any specific one, but had the feel of all of them. He took out his gun and checked his ammunition. He had two shots left. He said, "Pistol."

Kramer stopped and slowly turned, looking heroic. He was a handsome man with a full mustache and a rather large, eagle-like nose. "Yeah, kid?" George didn't particularly like being called "kid," but he let it go.

"I've got two shots. Is that gonna do us?"

Pistol reached into his vest, pulled out a gun, and handed it to George. "Here."

George took it and said, "Thank you." They resumed walking. The gun was a revolver with six shots—it looked like a cowboy pistol to George. Kramer's, he knew, was similar. Now that he thought about it, that other gun was completely out of place in this world; Kramer had seen it and hadn't said anything. And George's sweatshirt was equally out of place. Whatever. If Kramer wasn't worried about it, he wasn't going to worry about it.

They kept walking. About half a minute after Kramer had handed George the revolver there was a loud shriek above them. George turned and looked up—a large, shrieking red gorilla, arms and legs spread, was falling toward them—it would land on George. He jumped to the side. There was a loud gunshot. The animal slammed into the ground where he had been standing. He looked at it, then at Kramer, who was—with no particular expression—putting his gun back in its holster. "Be careful," Kramer said.

"Thanks."

George's heartbeat gradually slowed down to normal as they continued to walk. George noticed that the jungle ahead of them was changing. After a while Kramer stopped and held up his hand, and George stopped. Kramer: "This is it." He motioned George to come beside him, which George did. In front of them the land dropped dramatically. Below them in the distance was an ancient city, in ruins but still impressive, behind a great wall. In front of the wall the jungle had been cleared. The wall and most of the buildings were made of stone. The wall was about 15 feet high but was in ruins in many places. From where they were they could see no gate. The buildings varied so much from each other it was like they'd been randomly selected from all over the world and brought here. They varied in height as in every other way; the tallest, maybe five stories, rose to a level slightly higher than Kramer and George. Many of the roofs were gone; most of those still intact were domes. The largest building was a massive dome, maybe four stories tall at its center. George could see the sun, low in the sky in front of them—he now knew it was morning. With the sunlight reflecting off of it the ancient city was beautiful.

Kramer: "It's all ours, kid."

"Good. What's the plan?"

"No plan. We'll improvise. Follow me." He led George to a path that took them steeply downward, then on through the jungle. Eventually, they reached the place where the jungle had been cleared. The clearing indicated people stilled lived there. The two of them would be visible to anyone watching from within the city. George could see no one, of course, but he assumed someone was watching. He and Kramer, Kramer leading, ran across the clearing to a ruined area in the wall, a place where it rose only five feet. There were numerous places where the wall was lower, and one complete gap in the wall, several feet wide. "This should be safe," said Kramer, softly, and rapped the wall in several places with the machete. The last rap, of a stone at the top of the wall, caused a dart to shoot straight up from the stone. Kramer looked at George. "My mistake." He led George to a section of wall that was completely intact. George couldn't help reflecting that so far he'd played less of a role here than in any of the other worlds. But he wouldn't have complained even if Sullok had been there to complain to—he felt a little tense, but he was having fun. Kramer took a small grappling hook and rope out of his backpack, threw the hook to the top of the wall, pulled the rope taut, and climbed up. Near the top he rapped the wall with the machete; nothing happened. He pulled himself to the top of the wall, straddled it, and called George up. George hadn't climbed a rope in years, since he'd gone rock climbing with a few friends in his sophomore year in college. He climbed awkwardly at first, but quickly got the hang of it, and was soon sitting beside Kramer.

Kramer: "We want the big dome."

"Okay."

They used the rope to climb down the other side of the wall—Kramer first, then George. Then Kramer freed the grappling hook with a flick of the rope and returned the hook and rope to his backpack. Then they moved from building to building, hugging the walls, looking around for any watchers, hurrying though the open spaces. George sensed they were being watched and, since this was a movie, voiced his suspicion: "I think we're being watched."

Kramer, somewhat surprised: "See anyone?"

"No. Just a hunch."

"Well . . . keep looking. You might be right, but . . . I want that loot."

"Me too."

They reached the big dome. George, looking around, thought he saw someone out of the corner of his eye, in a window in a nearby building. He quickly turned to the window, but saw nothing. "Pistol," he said. "I think I saw someone."

"Where?"

Pointing: "There."

"You sure?"

"No."

"Alright. We better hurry."

The dome had no doors or windows that George could see. Kramer led him around it. George looked at the dome surface but saw only a stone wall, curving upwards. He also kept looking around for enemies but saw no one. He could still hear the jungle din in the background, though now it wasn't loud.

Suddenly Kramer stopped; George followed suit. Kramer was staring intently at the wall. To George it looked no different here than anywhere else. Placing his hands carefully, Kramer pushed. Nothing happened. He pushed harder, until he was straining. George pushed with him. Still nothing. Kramer: "A little to the left." George moved a little to the left, and pushed harder himself. Nothing at first, then the wall started to give a little. They kept pushing. The section of wall was a kind of revolving door—it revolved inward where they pushed. They moved quickly through the opening, and the section of wall, which had been moving so slowly, quickly swung back into position—Kramer narrowly missed being crushed. He said, in a low voice, "Good work, kid."

To George it was a great compliment. "Thanks, Pistol."

It was completely dark. George heard Kramer fumbling with something, then Kramer struck a match and used it to light a torch. They were in a stone corridor, roughly ten feet wide by ten feet high, with a little debris here and there but otherwise barren. The wall on the side through which they'd entered was curved, of course. The corridor stretched in either direction as far as the light traveled, though this wasn't far. It was at least a little cooler here than outside. They were both sweating. George mopped his forehead with the sleeve of his sweatshirt.

Kramer considered for a little while, then said, "This way," and took one of the two directions—there was no difference between them to George, who followed. Kramer, low: "Try not to talk. If you talk, keep your voice down." George answered with silence. They both stepped lightly and made very little noise. After about a minute Kramer held up a hand and they both stopped. Kramer studied the wall to their left, the one that wasn't curved. George did the same, but saw nothing. "Secret door," said Kramer. "You see the edge?" He held the torch near the wall.

George looked; to his surprise he could see a faint crack in the wall, covered with dust. "I see it."

"Here's the other side." Kramer moved the torch a few feet down the hall and held it up to the wall. Again George could see the faint crack. The door was about four feet wide. Kramer: "Push the top." They stood in front of it and pushed high. Nothing at first, then it started to move a little, then suddenly the top swung in and down as the bottom swung out and up. George almost yelled but caught himself. The door flipped upside down, with them riding it, and thus deposited them on the other side in a heap.

The torch was still burning. George grabbed it and they both stood up. They were in a similar corridor; this one formed the base of a T with the other. The air was more stale here. Kramer took the torch and led the way. After about 20 feet the passage started to go down. Not long after that it took a 90-degree turn. Kramer stopped and held his hand up again, and George stopped. Kramer looked around the corner. He waved George forward and, putting his finger to his lips, gestured for George to look. He did, and saw a hallway with reliefs of human figures—warriors, male and female, with a variety of weapons, and little clothing. There were small holes in the walls at their eyes. Some were standing, some kneeling, and some squatting. The floor continued to go steadily downward. He pulled back around the corner, and Kramer led him back a short distance the way they'd come.

Kramer: "It's a Glyssow Way. We need to be very quiet when we go through. Not a word. Don't touch the walls. And don't pass in front of the eyes. Got it?"

"And if we screw up?"

"Either of us makes a mistake, we're both dead in seconds. Fair enough?"

"Fine. Want me to lead?"

Kramer smiled. "You're okay, kid. Just follow me." They went to the corner; the reliefs began just beyond it. The reliefs on either side at any given place did not mirror each other, but the eyes were at the same level. Kramer moved past the first pair of warriors, then George followed, staying always one pair of warriors behind. The first warriors were standing upright; ducking under them was easy. The next were kneeling. Kramer and George had to crawl to get under their eyes. The next were standing. Then two were squatting, their faces fairly close to the ground. Kramer and then George stepped over the level of the eyes. George imagined red beams going out from the figures' eyes, and concentrated on not breaking the beams. He reflected that even here he was only imitating Kramer's actions, but he could live with that. If he got to choose his next scenario, he'd try to pick something that would put him in the center of the action. Why not? He caught himself and returned his attention to the reliefs—he didn't want this scenario to end. Squatting figures were the trickiest. He and Kramer did an odd, tense semi-dance through the Glyssow Way, which ran about 50 feet. At the end of it, after the last pair of warriors, an easy standing pair, Kramer jumped about three feet, and of course George did the same. Then Kramer turned and gently tapped the part of the floor they'd jumped across. A roughly two-foot section fell; after a surprisingly long period, George heard it strike the bottom. Kramer smiled and winked at him. He smiled and nodded, and they kept going.

The corridor continued to take them downward. George noticed the air was getting a little less stale, and it was getting a little cooler. Then he could see some light ahead. They slowed down and moved even more quietly. The light, weirdly, was purple. As they drew close, George could see that they were approaching an opening to a large chamber. He felt nervous and happy. There was a strange musky scent in the air, which grew stronger as they moved forward. The corridor continued to go downward.

They reached the opening and looked into it. They saw a huge chamber, roughly cylindrical, about 60 yards in diameter and 50 yards deep. They were near the top. A few dozen pots large enough to hold a man blazed with purple flames. At the far side of the chamber was a statue, maybe twenty feet tall and ten wide, of a squat, evil-looking creature which looked to be half human and half Gila monster; its pointed teeth were bared, and it wore a hateful expression. The statue was of a full body, but two-thirds of it was taken up with the creature's head. Around the statue were great piles of glittering treasure—mainly gems, jewels, and coins. There were openings to four passageways spaced evenly around the chamber at floor level.

Kramer, jutting his square jaw in the direction of the statue: "Mavri." He stepped through the opening; George did the same. They were on a rather narrow ledge. Kramer took his backpack off, took out the rope, and untied the grappling hook from the end. He found an outcropping, tied the rope to it, tested it, then put his backpack on again and climbed down. Once he'd reached the bottom, George climbed down after him.

The chamber looked different from this level, more impressive. They walked quickly and quietly to the treasure. Kramer: "I wish you hadn't lost your backpack." He took a large, empty cloth sack from his own backpack and handed it to George. "We need to move fast. You want jewelry over the rest, then gems. Let me get the artifacts."

George did as he was instructed, grabbing rings, necklaces, a small, jeweled book, bracelets, earrings, and other items, some of which he could not have identified. Kramer filled his backpack. There were odd items here and there—figurines, gadgets, little machines, items of clothing, other things, some of which Kramer took and some of which he left alone. George tested his bag occasionally to make sure it wasn't too heavy. When he was most of the way there he grabbed a few handfuls of gems and dropped those in as well. He got up, carrying the sack over his shoulder. Kramer was still on the floor, finishing. George heard footfalls. Kramer sprang to his feet. George dropped his bag, which hit the floor with a crash. Men ran into the chamber from all four openings. They looked like the relief figures. George remembered the reliefs and was grateful that none of these warriors were female. They wielded all manner of weapons, including clubs, axes, swords, knives, maces, spears, and war hammers. All at once they started a great war yell.

There were dozens of them in the chamber already, and they kept coming. Kramer turned, ran to the statue, and scrambled up its huge face. The yelling intensified. George followed, though he had more trouble climbing. Kramer pulled him up when he neared the top. The top of the statue was basically flat, which was a big help. Kramer: "This is it, kid." He fast-drew and started firing at the nearest warriors, who were quite close. Each shot killed a man.

George took out his *Hidden Agendas* gun. "It's been good, Pistol." A spear came at him; he twisted sideways and it merely grazed him, making a small tear in his sweatshirt, at the chest, and just breaking his skin. The warriors were climbing the statue. Their yelling was deafening. George shot the nearest warrior in the face, then shot another in the chest. Kramer kicked a man who'd almost reached the top, and sent the guy tumbling. George dropped his gun and pulled out the revolver. He was focusing on the nearest warriors, but there seemed to be an army in the chamber. They were climbing up the statue from all sides. Several were near the top now. He and Kramer were facing in opposite directions—he faced the statue's back. He shot the nearest warrior, cocked his revolver with his free hand, and shot another. A falling warrior would often knock down one or more of his comrades, but still they came faster than George could kill them. A few arrows flew; they all missed him. He cocked the revolver and shot another man. Then one actually had a foot on the statue's flat top; George shot and the man fell back. The next warrior made it with both feet to the top; George shot him and he fell, dying on the flat surface rather than falling off. Another appeared to replace him. George shot this man—his sixth shot. Not turning, he yelled to Kramer, "I'm out of bullets!" Another man was on top—George jumped at him feet first, and knocked him off. George landed on his feet, butt, and hands, but quickly popped back up, as two more reached the top on his side. One of these smiled, seeing him unarmed. Somehow Kramer was still firing; he must have had several guns. George grabbed the weapon, a club, of the warrior who died on the statue top. He swung it at the smiling warrior's head, and the man fell off. George turned and the other was on top of him, wielding a hammer. George ducked the hammer, jabbed the club into the man's stomach, then—as the man doubled over—swung it at his head and knocked him out. George turned and there was another foe. He heard Kramer yell, but couldn't afford to turn. "You okay?" His foe had an axe and a shield; George swung his club and the man easily blocked it with the shield.

Kramer, sounding wounded but determined: "I'm fine!"

They were screwed. It crossed George's mind that he was glad this wasn't real. He swung the club again and his opponent cut it neatly in two, then laughed. George turned—there was another man. In desperation, he ran at the new man, screaming. Out of the corner of his eye, he could see the man who'd cut his club, then the man's shield, coming fast, then darkness.

He woke up in the same chamber, at the base of the statue, looking up. He was happy to be in the same adventure. His wrists and ankles were bound by ropes, his arms over his head, his legs spread-eagled. He was on what appeared to be a stone table. He looked around as best he could. Kramer, unconscious, was tied to a stone table in the same manner. Around them were many warriors, male and female. The treasure had been cleared away from their immediate area, and there was a white circle a few feet in diameter painted on the floor of the chamber. He noticed that even the warriors with treasure all around them seemed to ignore it. Now that he had time to think about it, he didn't like that he'd been killing natives. He'd been defending himself, but from what he actually knew, he and Kramer were in the wrong—they'd come here to steal the natives' treasure.

On the other hand, since this was a Pistol Kramer movie, the natives as a group had to be guilty of doing lots of very bad things. But in a way that was the problem. If this were an actual movie, people would complain about the racial and cultural implications—the story was set up so that the black natives were the bad guys, and the white outsiders who came and killed a lot of them were the good guys. George would have watched the movie and enjoyed it, but he would have thought the people making those complaints had a point.

Sullok was nearby, wearing a long black robe with a jeweled belt. His hair for once was not in a ponytail. Around his neck he wore a small brown leathery bag. Next to him was a woman almost as tall, with long blond hair teased out, a dark green robe, gray belt with a dagger in a scabbard, fingernails painted black, full lips painted yellow, large blue eyes, a stern expression on her face. George was actually happy to see Sullok. In all the excitement he hadn't thought much about the fellow, but it stood to reason he'd show up. "Hi, Sullok."

Sullok, expressionless, looked down at him. "What did you say?"

"I said 'hi.'"

"My name is Nikolas."

"Nikolas. Okay." George was in a good mood. He looked over at Kramer. The hero's backpack was gone and his holster was empty, but he still had his fedora on. George thought about waking him, then decided he should talk to Sullok first. He turned his head back toward the man. "Listen, thanks for bringing me here. It's been great. I've had a ball. I'd like to stay a while if that's okay."

Sullok smiled, not unkindly. "I'm afraid that's not possible."

The woman said, harshly, in a heavy German accent, "What are you talking about?"

Sullok, gently: "It's alright, mistress." That seemed to satisfy her; she turned away and spoke in a low voice to a female warrior.

George: "For my next adventure, I'd like . . . ." He hadn't thought much about it; he'd been too busy. But he wanted to put in a request now that he had an opportunity. "I'd like to be a superhero. One that can fly." That might be fun. He'd think about it more carefully next time.

Sullok looked a little unhappy. "I'm sorry." He turned away and went to the woman.

George frowned. He turned to Kramer. "Pistol! Wake up!" Kramer began to stir. George repeated, "Wake up!" and Kramer awakened completely. He looked around, assessing his situation.

Finally Kramer said: "Nice to see you, kid. I figured that was sayonara back there." He looked around again. "It could get a little tricky from here."

George smiled. He had no fear he and Kramer were about to die.

That would never happen in a Pistol Kramer movie. He as an individual was at some risk—a sidekick might be killed. He said, "Yeah, it, it could take a little finesse." Kramer laughed.

The woman turned so she was facing the warriors. "Back! Back!" she hissed at them, and they complied. Once they'd given her plenty of room, she lifted her arms into a V and said, in a tone meant to be solemn, but sounding almost comical to George: "Minions of Mavri. The time has come. These fools came to steal from Mavri. They now lie helpless. We could kill them at once, but that is not the way of Mavri." She paused, then hissed: "The bones!" The warriors roared their approval.

She lowered her arms and turned to Sullok, who moved toward her. He reached into the bag around his neck, took out two black and white objects that George couldn't quite make out, and handed them to her. She turned back to the warriors and held up her arms again, one of the objects in each hand. She yelled: "The bones!" The warriors roared even louder. Then she lowered her arms and tossed the objects toward the white circle. The objects were in fact small bones; they bounced and rolled and eventually came to a stop inside the circle. Each was a few inches long and had knobby ends. One half of each bone was painted black. On the black half of each were white dots; on the white half were black dots. There was silence for a moment, as everyone who could see them looked at the bones. Then the woman dramatically unsheathed the dagger and held it over her head. "Minions of Mavri. The bones have spoken. The time has come to feed our master . . . with blood!" She waved the dagger. The warriors gave the loudest roar yet.

George tested his bonds—whoever had tied him had done a fine job. He looked over at Kramer, who was struggling with his own bonds and getting nowhere. How were they going to get out of this?

The woman walked toward them; she seemed to flow. The warriors became totally quiet. She stopped between the two stone tables and waved the dagger once more. She looked at George, then Kramer. Her eyes rested on Kramer. "I am Amita, high priestess of Mavri, Mavri the Invincible!" The warriors gasped. "These two beautiful specimens . . . ." Her eyes had remained on Kramer; she looked him up and down. "Beautiful . . . but doomed—they shall feed our master." Her voice had fallen; it rose again: "He shall drink their blood, and eat their hearts!" She lifted her arms dramatically, and the warriors kneeled.

She was still looking at Kramer. Her face was no longer stern; she looked confused. Kramer looked up at her courageously. She hesitated. Then she brought the dagger down swiftly to the center of his chest. She stopped with the blade just touching him. She paused there, then clenched her jaw and raised the dagger again. "You must all show respect!" she cried angrily. "Look at the ground, all of you! You also, Nikolas!" George, straining his neck a little, saw the warriors do as she'd commanded, though their faces showed confusion. Sullok, his face blank, did the same.

Then, moving quickly and skillfully, Amita cut the ropes at Kramer's wrists, then those at his ankles. "Come," she whispered urgently, taking his hand. He took the dagger from her—she didn't resist—then swung to a sitting position, hopped lightly off the table, went to George, and cut him free. Kramer winked at him again.

George smiled. He got off the table as quietly as he could, though not as quietly as Kramer had. Amita motioned for them to follow her; she had a torch in one hand now—she led them around to the back of the statue, opened a narrow, concealed door in it, and led them through the opening. George went through last; as he did, he heard Sullok yell: "Warriors! Annihilate them!"

The door opened to a set of steep, narrow stairs—George rushed down them, following the others. Amita's torch was the only light. As he reached the bottom of the stairs he could hear their pursuers at the top. George, Kramer, and Amita were in a narrow stone tunnel. George ran as fast as he could, but could not keep up with the others. The light was still terrible—there was just her torch and a few torches in the hands of the warriors. He didn't like it here, though he wasn't angry with Sullok, or whoever or whatever was responsible for his being here. The tunnel went on for hundreds of yards. Kramer: "Hurry, kid!"

George pushed himself harder. He looked back—they were gaining on him. The closest was less than ten yards back. Amita, to George: "Faster!" She herself was very fast despite the robe she wore.

George was slowing them down. He just wasn't in good enough shape to hold his own in the race. "Don't wait for me!"

They were pulling away from him, though Kramer kept looking back. Kramer: "It's not much further! Give it all you got!" George didn't know what he meant, but he groaned and pushed himself to his limit. Still he could hear the bad guys getting closer. It would've helped if he'd genuinely feared for his life. Then Kramer and Amita opened a door to a lighted room and ran in. He hadn't expected this. The warriors were on top of him, but maybe he could make it. He felt something pierce his back; he kept running.

He ran into the room, and heard the door slam behind him. A warrior had come in on his heels. George turned and hit him. The man, who was running into the punch, jerked his head aside at the last moment but still caught part of it on his chin. He crashed to the floor, his sword flying out of his hand. The sword was red with George's blood.

George realized he was in pain. He sat down on the floor. He looked at the others. Kramer had stuck the dagger in his belt. Amita stepped toward him and drew the dagger out. Now Kramer looked confused.

There was a wooden bar across the door. The warriors were pounding on it from the other side. Amita moved calmly to the warrior, who was unconscious, and slit his throat. She showed not even a trace of remorse.

Kramer knelt beside George. George tried to stand but couldn't. He fell into Kramer's arms. He laughed. This was too much.

Amita: "He's done. We must run—the door will not contain them."

Kramer ignored her. "How you feel, kid?"

George smiled. "I've been better." He could barely move, but the pain was relatively mild.

Amita was at the other end of the room, in front of an open door. "My love! We must flee!"

Kramer looked up at her and snapped: "Go! I'll catch up! This is my friend!"

Her tone changed abruptly, becoming tender: "I understand. But do not wait too long. Your friend does not want you to die. Do you, 'kid?'"

"No." George considered thanking her, but decided to let it go. He appreciated what she'd done for them, but she was basically an evil woman.

She said, "I'll be waiting out there, so you can say goodbye to your friend." She walked through the doorway.

Kramer looked down at George. "So what do you think? Make a good wife?"

George laughed, and this briefly sharpened the pain. "Sure. Great wife. Listen, it's been great knowing you. You better go. Like the lady said."

Kramer laughed, sadly. " 'Lady.' " He shook his head. He was playing up George's joke. "Listen, I hate to leave you, kid."

"It's okay. Screw 'em. I'm okay. I'm . . . I'm going on an amazing adventure." George had been caught up in the moment, but he wondered now what would happen to Kramer when he, George, died. George was fairly sure he himself would go on to another world. Kramer, he suspected, faced oblivion. "Actually, I worry about you."

Kramer shook his head, and chuckled. "Just like you." Then he lay George down.

"Goodbye, Pistol."

Kramer picked up the sword, then looked down at George. He blinked and wiped one of his eyes. "I won't let them kill you." His voice was choked. He raised the sword over George's neck.

George nodded. It was all too much. "It's okay. Do it. Goodbye, Pistol."

"Goodbye, kid." The sword came down.

# CHAPTER 5

George felt a little choked up as he appeared in his new world, so it was a little slow to register with him. It was overwhelmingly barren. He stood in front of a man and a woman sitting across from each other at a table. Around them was a remarkably empty landscape; he saw very little vegetation. The two sat in the middle of a crossroads. The roads themselves were little more than dirt, and little different from the land around them, but he could easily make out the roads' edges. Each road had a pair of wheel tracks going through it, but no vehicles were visible in any direction. The table was inside a square formed by the crossing wheel tracks. George could see a long way in every direction, but saw only the roads, absolutely straight, and the barren land around them. The sun was visible, along with blue sky and just a few wispy clouds. The temperature was in the seventies. There was an open treasure chest, like you'd see in a pirate movie but smaller, off the roads in a corner created by their intersection.

The man looked to be in his late thirties, with brown hair and beard, no mustache, balding, wearing blue jeans, a white T-shirt, and red sneakers. The woman looked to be in her late twenties, with blond hair in a pixie cut, glasses, wearing yellow jeans, a powder blue T-shirt with some kind of illustration on it, and red sneakers. The man looked to George like a blue-collar worker; the woman had an intellectual look. The table and chairs were wooden and simple but looked sturdy. Under the table was a worn-looking gray carpetbag. The man was looking at George. The woman said: "Don't look! That's what he wants!"

George realized now that his back no longer hurt. It hadn't since he'd been in this world. He was glad about that, but he definitely did not want to be here. He said, "Minimalism."

"What did he say?" asked the man urgently, still looking at George.

She answered, "He said 'minimalism,' you fool!" She was still looking at the man.

George recognized this. It was *A Man and a Woman at a Crossroads*, by William Bagby, by far the most famous minimalist playwright. This was his big play. George had never seen it, but he'd read it a few years ago, for a class. He'd been impressed by it but found it unpleasant. He couldn't remember the names of these two characters. "Hi," he said.

"What'd he say?" said the man, now looking at the woman.

She stood up, angry. "Why do you ask me what he said?"

He looked down. "I don't know." He looked up. "Who else should I ask?"

George rolled his eyes. He looked around and yelled, "Sullok!"

Woman: "He said, 'Sullok.'"

Man, standing: "I heard him, woman! I'm no fool! We should help him!"

Woman: "Sullok!"

Man: "Sullok!"

Woman, to George: "Maybe we should yell together."

George: "Let it go. Thanks, though."

Woman, puzzled: "'Thanks, though?'"

Man: "You're welcome."

George was surprised this was going as well as it was. From what he remembered of the play, he'd have expected conversation with these two to be torture. It wasn't quite that bad, so far.

Woman, to man: "We could leave with him."

This surprised George momentarily; then he remembered they *talked* about leaving a good deal.

Man: "What if he doesn't want us to?" He sat back in his chair.

George, enthusiastic: "I *do* want you to! You should both come with me!" He was fairly sure they wouldn't. Neither of them left in the play, even for a minute. Furthermore, even though he didn't want them with him, if they did come it'd be worth it to him just to see them leave this place.

Man, irritated: "But *I* don't want to leave."

Woman: "Why don't you want to leave?"

George noticed the treasure chest again. He walked over to it. He could see the front of her T-shirt now: there was a cheerful illustration of a kitten on it. He knew the play was written in the '40s or '50s; the shirt was obviously from a later era.

Man: "Do I need a reason?"

Woman: "You could have a reason."

George looked in the chest—it was empty. He frowned and took a deep breath.

# ADVENTURE

Man: "I just don't want to. Does that count as a reason?"
Woman: "No."

The man said, "You could leave with . . . ." but George cut him off.

George: "Have you seen a tall thin man with long blond hair?"

The man's brow furrowed. He turned to the woman, who at that moment sat down again. He asked, "Have we seen a tall thin man with long blond hair?"

George was irritated with himself for asking. "Forget it!"

Woman, to man: "We haven't seen anyone!"

George: "Goodbye." He turned his back on them and started down the nearest road. Behind him, he heard the man say, "Well, now he's leaving."

Woman: "Good. I never liked him."

George stopped, stood there a moment, then turned and walked back. They both watched him. When he was back in the crossroads, he said, angrily: "One: fuck you. Two: it's not the world that's empty and pointless, it's this play." He turned again and strode off.

Behind him, he heard her ask, in a wounded tone, "What did he mean by that?"

The man answered: "Ha! His meaning is self-evident!" Then they were silent.

George kept walking. A few steps later he heard her say something, softly, which he wasn't close enough to make out. That was fine. Whatever she had said, the man answered, "Nonsense!" Then George could hear their voices but make nothing out, then he couldn't hear them at all. He remembered reading, on the back of a paperback edition of the play, a quote from a novelist—he couldn't remember who it was, but he remembered it was one he liked—claiming that *A Man and a Woman at a Crossroads* was the only convincing love story ever written. Whoever had written it, it was pretty stupid. He took another deep breath and smiled. He felt good. He promised himself he would not go back to them. Whoever or whatever guided this might find a way to bring them together again, but he would not return voluntarily. Now he could remember their names: John and Johnna.

He had felt almost no wind since he arrived. All he seemed to have here was the road and barren land. He could still see John and Johnna if he looked back, but that was no consolation. They were bleaker than the landscape. He looked up. The sky still looked cheerful. It occurred to him that a lot of people would look down on him, a Ph.D. candidate in American Literature, for enjoying the Pistol Kramer world but hating this one. But, he reflected, those people hadn't had to talk to John and Johnna. He appreciated the play; he just didn't want to live in it.

He wondered where else they would take him. He had a vague notion in his head of people sitting around a table, sleeves rolled up, ties loosened, late at night, throwing out ideas on where to send him next. It was ludicrous, of course, but he couldn't help thinking of it like that. He imagined reptilian aliens and then blobs of energy gathered in futuristic rooms, doing basically the same thing, which seemed even more ludicrous. Whoever it was, what would they do for their next world? He said, not sure whom he was quoting: "We shot the last act in the first reel."

He didn't know how he'd handle Sullok when the guy inevitably turned up. He would have said in the Pistol Kramer world that he owed Sullok one for that, but *this* world was terrible. Obviously he could be in worse situations. He could be in a war movie, wounded and in pain. That didn't make him grateful, however, any more than he would be grateful to a mugger who refrained from hitting him. He hadn't asked to be here. He had stepped into the first world, but that didn't amount to asking for all of this. On the other hand, he didn't regret that step, in spite of everything. Surely, the opportunity he'd had then would never have come again. And if he hadn't gone through the doorway he'd have always been kicking himself for not going through. He'd get up in the morning, drink coffee, go to work, maybe be married and have kids, grow old, and he'd always go back to thinking about the time the doorway had opened and he hadn't walked through it.

There was so little change in the landscape, such as it was, that once John and Johnna were no longer visible he almost felt as if he wasn't moving, as if he was on a great treadmill. Furthermore, he was hungry. He hadn't eaten since all of this began.

He wouldn't be surprised if he reached John and Johnna again, magically, by continuing to walk forward. If that happened, as soon as he was sure it was them he would walk a diagonal path to the other road, ignoring them even if they spoke to him, and follow the other road. If that led back to them he would leave the roads and walk in a random direction. He wouldn't let whoever was doing this break him. Or if he did break, it wouldn't be easy for them. He could just walk away from the road now, of course, but he didn't want to do that.

A while later, he had to stop to piss. Quite a while after that, about an hour after he'd left John and Johnna—a long time in these circumstances—he could barely make something out on the road ahead of him. It was little more than a speck. He assumed it was Sullok. Though it would be typical of these worlds for his expectation to prove false. Nevertheless, it looked more and more like Sullok as he drew closer. He thought about how he would handle the situation. He decided he'd play it by ear. Now he was sure it was Sullok. The man was wearing blue jeans, a navy blue T-shirt, red sneakers, and the ponytail. He was smoking a cigar.

It took a while for the two to reach one another. As they got closer to each other, neither of them said anything. When they were maybe ten feet apart, Sullok took the cigar out of his mouth. He wasn't smiling exactly but he looked friendly. George stopped in front of him, blocking his path. George's face was expressionless. He'd let Sullok speak first.

Sullok smiled, nodded, returned the cigar to his mouth, and stepped around him.

This pissed George off. He grabbed Sullok's shoulder and spun him around. George: "Why am I here? What's your point?"

The cigar stayed put. Sullok spoke around it. "No point."

"Are you gonna talk in minimalist dialogue?"

Short pause. "I'm gonna talk."

"Fine. Me too."

Sullok took the cigar out of his mouth again. No smile, but a pleasant expression. "Talk."

"Are you playing some kind of character? Are we going to do it that way?"

"I'm me."

"You're you. That doesn't mean anything. Let's do it like this—do you know who Sullok is?"

"No."

"Liar."

Sullok turned, in no hurry, and started to walk away.

George took a step in that direction, then stopped. "Okay." He turned around and walked the other way. He said over his shoulder, emphatically: "Fuck you. I'll keep walking till I drop if that's what if takes. I won't play ball." Then he faced forward again, never stopping. There was nothing new to see. That didn't matter. He wouldn't cave in. He was tempted to look back, but he didn't.

He heard Sullok say, "You win." Then everything vanished.

## CHAPTER 6

George was sitting in the passenger's seat of a large convertible. He blinked. There had been no discernable interval between the Bagby world and this one. He turned to the driver, a small thin man, bald, wearing sunglasses and a baseball cap, smoking a pipe. The man was talking: ". . . So I shot the bastard. What was I supposed to do?" The guy wore tan walking shorts, a red basketball jersey, and cowboy boots. He continued: "I didn't kill him, you understand. Just shot him in the gut." He nodded. "You shoot a man in the gut, he remembers."

George looked around. They were on a two-lane highway in another desert, but this one seemed real, with plenty of shrubs, mountains in the distance, and features in the landscape instead of an almost completely flat plain. Actually, this seemed quite different from the world George was just in. He glanced at the speedometer—they were doing just under 80. The radio was playing a rock and roll song he didn't recognize.

Driver: "What'd you say?"

George: "I didn't say anything." The world seemed somewhat familiar.

Driver, yelling: "Bullshit!" The car swerved sickeningly from side to side.

George was afraid the driver would lose control and crash. Then he remembered he'd probably just go on to the next world. And it was a movie, or whatever. Then the swerving stopped. George: "You're an asshole."

The driver laughed uproariously, which didn't surprise George. The car again swerved from side to side, and again the driver got it back under control.

George considered asking to be let out. He doubted the guy would do it, but he could ask anyway on general principles. He didn't though; he didn't want to do even that until he figured out what this world was. He asked, "Who are you?"

The driver laughed again, not as hard. "George, you are going to have to tone it down. Cut back on the tequila, cut back on the cocaine, cut back on something. I don't know. Maybe become an Episcopalian priest or Lindsey's ambassador to Belgium."

Now George had it. The man was "Professor" Panama T. Johnson, the best-known "hit and run" journalist. This was the beginning of *Beyond Las Vegas*, which was about a week Johnson spent in Las Vegas in 1971 with his "physician," a small Japanese man who shared Johnson's love of excess. Johnson was supposedly there to cover the North-Fernandez heavyweight title fight for *Journey* magazine, but the two of them spent the entire week taking drugs, behaving oddly, and abusing whomever happened to be around them, and Johnson wrote primarily about that. They didn't even go to the fight, though Johnson caught part of one round on a television set in a whorehouse. George had read the book, called a nonfiction novel, a few years ago; he'd finished it in less than a day. However, the final scene—in which Johnson and his partner dragged a middle-aged waitress out of a diner and threw her into a dumpster, because she had refused to serve them toast—had offended him so much that as soon as he'd finished the book he'd torn it up and thrown it away. A friend of his he always saw at Javaland, the Sawyerville coffeehouse he liked, was a big fan of Johnson and had read most of his books. George didn't mind hearing about it, but dealing one on one with Johnson was another matter. And he was obviously cast in the role of the physician, which made it worse.

Johnson: "Here, take the wheel." He let go of the steering wheel; George grabbed it. Johnson then turned and climbed into the backseat. George carefully slid over into the driver's seat as the car decelerated. It had fallen well below the speed limit by the time he was in place; he brought it up to 70. Johnson: "Faster!"

"No."

Johnson didn't respond. George glanced in the rearview mirror and saw that his companion was rifling through an old, beaten-up suitcase. George's eyes returned to the road. After a while Johnson climbed back into the front seat. The car's interior was maroon. George had to admit he liked the car.

Johnson said, "Here, take this," and tried to hand George a red pill.

"Pass."

"Pass! Pass! You android! The sun is cooking your brain!" Johnson swallowed the pill himself. Then he uncapped a bottle of dark rum and took a drink. "I think you need some acid." He reached into the back seat.

"I don't think so."

Johnson sighed. "Some milk? A beer?"

"That I can do." He hadn't driven with an open beer in the car in years. He kind of liked the idea. He could get away with anything here. He didn't *want* to get away with much, right now, but a beer would be good. Beyond that, he was hungry, but he wasn't going to ask Johnson for food.

Johnson climbed into the back seat again. The wind was intense, but he didn't seem to notice.

George felt cold metal touch his neck. He reached back and took it, then looked to see what it was—a can of Fritz's. He held it with the hand he had on the steering wheel and pulled the tab with the other. The tab was the kind that came off, of course. He hadn't seen one of those in years. He took a drink. It tasted good; the coldness of it was the best part. He relaxed a little. He wondered how long it had been in personal time since he'd walked into the rainy city. Getting killed there had taken relatively little time, but he'd had a long stay in the *Hidden Agendas* world—he'd even gone to sleep. Then maybe half an hour in the Xerxi world. Then a while in the Pistol Kramer world, including being unconscious for an indeterminate length of time, probably not long, then over an hour in the Bagby world, most of it walking in an empty desert. Maybe he could get away from Johnson and then rest for a while in this world. Unfortunately, he didn't have enough money for a hotel room. Johnson would get them one, but then he'd have to deal with Johnson. He took another drink.

Johnson climbed into the front seat again. "I don't know what's gotten into you, but you're going to have to drive faster or we'll never make it. Either that or pull over and let me drive."

"When do we have to be there?"

"Three o'clock or we'll lose our reservation."

"What time is it?"

Johnson, dramatically: "Barbarian! What's the purpose of these questions? This experience is not linear!" When George didn't respond, Johnson said in a calmer tone, "It was past noon when I ate the mushrooms."

Why couldn't he just say what time it was? "So it's what? Before 12:30?"

Johnson just grunted.

"We passed a sign a while back that said, 'Las Vegas, 110 Miles.' I'm doing 70. We'll make it."

"You fool!" Johnson took the pipe out of his mouth and hurled it at George's head. George ducked but it hit him anyway—the impact was surprisingly unpleasant. He threw his beer at Johnson, who successfully dodged it. Johnson continued: "What kind of reasoning is that? You sicken me!" George pulled the car over. Johnson grabbed George's neck and started to choke him. George first focused on getting the car completely stopped and shifting to park, then tried to pry Johnson's hands away. Johnson, climbing on top of him: "You lunatic! This is for your own good! I'd do this for my brother if I had one!" Johnson was stronger than he looked, but still relatively weak. George got Johnson's hands away from his neck, then raised himself up so he had a knee on the seat and pushed Johnson back to the passenger's side. Johnson: "For the love of Jesus what's wrong with you?" George hit him in the nose as hard as he could. He heard a popping sound and saw blood. Johnson looked genuinely surprised. Then George stepped over the seat, onto the back seat, then onto the trunk, across the trunk, and onto the gravel of the road's shoulder. Johnson: "I can't believe you hit me! You're my doctor!"

George just kept walking. He didn't look back. He'd never have done that in a real desert, but this wasn't real. He didn't want to be with Johnson in that confined space all the way to Vegas, and he had no use for the man once they got there. Nor, for that matter, did he particularly want to be in Vegas. He wondered how Johnson would handle his behavior. He couldn't imagine the man walking after him, pleading with him to get back in the car. Then he heard Johnson yell, "Forgive me, brother!" and drive away, gunning the engine. He still didn't look back.

It hadn't taken long. He was walking in the desert again. But it was a better desert, and he had a little wind. This desert wasn't real, but it seemed real, and that was good enough. He considered turning around, but thought that would be lame. It didn't matter, anyway. Vegas was the other way, but Vegas wasn't the nearest town, and he didn't know in which direction the nearest town lay. Actually, the Vegas direction was probably a better bet, but screw it. It was all academic, anyway. He wouldn't be walking long before Sullok arrived. The heat was the worst part—that was the one thing that really bothered him at the moment.

1971. It was the year before he was born. He thought about what his parents were doing. His sister Ginny was alive; she'd be about two years old. It was nice to think of her at that age. The three years difference had meant less and less as they'd grown older, but she'd always sort of had seniority. They'd gotten along well, though; they'd seldom fought, even when they were little, and they were pretty close now. She was a lawyer and lived in Chicago. He thought about calling his parents, just to see how they would react. He wouldn't consider it if he were really somehow in 1971, but this wasn't real.

Then it all caught up with him. What the hell was going on? Nothing terrible had happened so far, in a sense, but the walls of reality had come down, and that was terrible enough. He didn't feel that bad; he wasn't panicking. But this was all absurd. He again felt angry at whoever was doing this. He could blow off Sullok when the guy showed up. On the other hand, should he? Abruptly, he decided to give Sullok one more chance. When he arrived, George would try to play ball. He expected Sullok to talk in code; he would do the same.

He crossed the highway—so he was walking with the traffic—stuck his thumb out, and kept moving. The first vehicle, a big red pickup truck, stopped for him. The driver wasn't Sullok. Whoever was doing this, they were continuing to surprise him. The driver was a white-haired elderly man wearing a cowboy hat. He said, "Hop in." George climbed inside, and they pulled away.

The radio played twangy country music, loud. Driver: "Where ya headed?"

George: "Wherever. Nowhere, really." Both windows were down. Between that and the music, they had to more or less yell at each other.

Driver: "Okay." He didn't say anything else.

George: "Thanks for picking me up."

Driver: "Well, I don't mind. It's the least I could do, you bein' in the desert and all."

Neither of them said anything else. The old man seemed like a nice guy, but George didn't want to talk. The old man didn't seem to want to either, and in any event he wasn't real. In real life George would've asked where the driver was going, but here he didn't bother. Now that he'd left Johnson, he doubted he'd be here long. And he hadn't stayed in any of these worlds for even a day, anyway, as far as he could tell. Would all this time be gone when he got back to Sawyerville? Maybe, maybe not. Of course, this was an incredible, once-in-a-lifetime adventure, for what that was worth. And that was another problem, looked at from a different angle—the rest of his life, if he got back to his life in Sawyerville, would seem dull by comparison. Furthermore, if he didn't find out what was going on, and maybe if he did, the unreality of this experience would always taint the real world around him. Nevertheless, he still didn't regret stepping through the doorway into the rainy city.

The old man drove about 60. Occasionally he sang along with the radio. That was fine. After a few songs George heard a siren. He looked back and saw a black XGQ with a small red rotating light above the driver. The old man said, "Shit," and pulled over.

George watched the XGQ pull over, and saw that the driver was Sullok. Sullok got out of the car, casually, turned off the rotating light, tossed it back in the car, and strutted toward them. His hair was in a ponytail; he wore sunglasses, a black jacket of some velvety material, a violet shirt, tight black pants in the same material, and red boots. To George he looked like a hipster undercover cop in a '70s TV show. *Beyond Las Vegas* had mentioned cool cops. He went to George's side of the truck. The old man turned off the radio. Sullok, hands on hips, to George: "Could you step out of the car, sir?"

George felt the urge to make a sarcastic remark, but fought it off—he wanted to play along this time. He opened the door and jumped to the ground. Sullok: "Are you George Preston?"

"Yes."

"My name's Joe Reed. I was hoping you could help me with an investigation. Would you mind coming with me?"

"No problem."

"Great." Sullok addressed the old man though the passenger window. "Thank you for stopping, sir. I'm a police detective. The man you picked up is going to help me with an investigation." The old man said something and held up a hand, then the truck pulled away.

Sullok said, "This way, sir," and strutted back in the direction of his car. George followed. They got into the car, which seemed new, and buckled their seatbelts. Sullok did a U-turn, and then asked, dropping the impersonal tone: "You know a guy named Panama Johnson?"

"Yes."

"And when did you last see him?" He drove fairly fast. The car had a very smooth ride.

George was happy to stick it to Johnson. "Maybe fifteen minutes ago. Headed for Vegas on this road. In a black Carmenita." He wanted to add, "You probably passed him," but didn't.

"I see. Were you with him?"

"Yes. We got into an argument, and I got out of the car."

"Hmm .... About what?"

"He was acting like a lunatic. I didn't want to deal with him."

"And why were you with him in the first place?"

George thought about it, then said, "That's kind of hard to answer."

Sullok hesitated. "What do you mean?"

"I mean I'm not sure why I was with him. I'm kind of confused about it myself."

"Hmmph."

George waited a while, then said, "A lot of strange things have been happening to me lately."

"What do you mean?"

"Well. It's hard to explain. It's like my whole world keeps changing. Know what I mean?"

Again Sullok hesitated. "Sort of."

"Yeah. Say, you wouldn't know anything about that, would you? Would it have anything to do with what you're investigating?" He was beginning to feel like he was kissing the guy's ass.

"Uh, maybe."

"Could you give me some idea what you're investigating?"

"I can't do that, man."

"Well, can you tell me anything?"

"Maybe. What do you want to know?"

"Well, I'd like to know what's going on."

"That's hard to answer."

"I see." This didn't seem to be getting George anywhere. He waited the guy out. The car had a new car smell. The interior was red and sharp-looking.

"Do you know where in Vegas Johnson's going?"

"I don't know the hotel. He was going to Vegas for the North-Fernandez fight."

"Thanks. You're being awfully cooperative."

"Yeah, well, I don't like the guy."

"Even though you were with him."

"That's right." George fought his annoyance. He seemed to be doing all the work.

"Do you know of any crimes he's committed? Or is planning to commit?"

"Nothing serious." This was too much—George wasn't going to detail Johnson's crimes, most of which were victimless anyway.

Sullok stayed on him: "Maybe I should be the judge of that."

"Nothing serious as far as I'm concerned. I don't want to discuss it. Good luck catching him."

The man sighed. "Thanks." Neither of them spoke for a few minutes. Every so often they'd pass a car or truck going the other way. Less often, they'd meet a vehicle in their lane; when this happened, Sullok would always smoothly accelerate and pass it. George figured he himself had more or less cut off the Johnson questions. But Sullok had gone too far—George hadn't had much choice. Finally Sullok asked, "So what are you gonna do?"

"I don't know." He considered a moment, then added, "Any suggestions?"

Sullok laughed. "I don't think so."

George thought, asshole. He said, "So how long you been on this case?"

"A while."

George was about to ask, "How long a while?" but he didn't. He clenched and relaxed his jaw muscles. "Fuck *this*." He took a deep breath. "Look," he said, then he didn't say anything for a while. Then he just said, "Screw it."

"Man, what's your problem?"

George stared out the window. The scenery was great. Then he turned to Sullok. "My problem, you fucking buffoon, is that I don't want to play this game anymore...."

"What game?"

"Shut the fuck up. You are going to shut up and listen to this, and I don't want to hear a goddam thing you have to say unless you want to cut the crap and give me direct answers. I walked out of my apartment—well, sort of—into an alternate reality. Then five more alternate realities, in succession, and I don't think the next one's far off. You've been in every one of them, but with a different name every time, if you gave me a name, and you never acknowledge any reality but the one we're in at the time. You hint around and talk in code, and even then you don't tell me anything. I ask you direct questions, you don't help. I try to play your fucking game, you don't help. Well I'm done playing. I didn't ask for this. I didn't choose it, not really, and I'm not gonna play anymore. Do what you want. What I want is to have nothing to do with you, you prick, and that is exactly what I'm going to do." He turned and watched the desert again.

Sullok just drove for a while. Finally he said: "I'll drive you out of the desert, anyway. You are one strange dude." He turned on the radio. It was a hip rock group of the era, the Mirrors. After that was a song by a group George didn't recognize, but they sounded about as hip. After a while, he fell asleep.

# CHAPTER 7

George woke up in relative darkness. He could tell, however, that it was a nice family living room. He was lying on a couch. There was a quilt on top of him. He tossed it on the floor and got up, then turned on a lamp and looked around. It was reminiscent of a living room in a late-'50s family sitcom. The television had an antenna. He kind of liked the place, but he wouldn't want to live here.

It was dark outside. A wall clock told him it was a little after 1:00 a.m. He was still wearing the clothes he'd had on in Sawyerville, and he realized he was dirty and starting to smell bad. And he needed a shave. Despite himself he felt like he was soiling this nice room. Was this his house? Surely it was a house, not an apartment. Fifties sitcom families tended to live in houses, especially if their rooms were like this. Was someone going to come down in pajamas and a robe, waving a golf club at him? Was his wife going to come down and ask what was wrong? Well, he could deal with whatever when it happened.

He decided he should try to wash his clothes. He risked, he supposed, getting chased out of the house naked, but he could deal with that. He looked for a washing machine. The next room was the kitchen. It looked too modern to be late-'50s, though it still had a little of that flavor. Seeing the refrigerator reminded him he was hungry. He opened it—it was full of inviting packages. He took out lunchmeat, milk, and squeezable mustard, found bread in a cabinet, and made himself a few sandwiches at the otherwise clean kitchen table. He drank out of the half-gallon plastic bottle. When he was done he put everything away and moved on. He went down a set of stairs to a cluttered basement—there was his washing machine, looking modern enough. This was probably a modern-day world, even though it was quaint.

He took off his clothes and threw them in the washer, then poured in soap and started it. Then he noticed his chest had healed. He'd gotten a small wound when the spear grazed him in the Pistol Kramer world; there was no trace of it now. His back had been wounded twice—twisting himself, he felt his back with his hands, and it felt normal. Interesting. Well, anyway, he needed a shower. He definitely took dirt with him from world to world. He left his sneakers and his wallet on the floor next to the washing machine. There was no bathroom in the basement, so he went back upstairs. He felt a little apprehensive walking around this place naked, and now with his clothes on another floor. He felt comfortable in his own apartment naked, but this was a completely different situation. Even if he was in the role of whoever lived here, the man of the house probably didn't wander around naked very much. But screw it—he'd been through the wringer, and he didn't care much what anyone here thought.

There was a bathroom on the first floor, with a tub, but he wanted a shower. He climbed another set of stairs and found another bathroom. The bathroom door was the only one he saw open. He suspected the bedrooms were up here, and there was almost certainly at least one other person in the house, but he could deal with that later. He went into the bathroom—it had a shower. He closed the door, turned on the water, found shampoo, soap, and a wash cloth, and took a shower. It was a great relief getting himself clean. He was drying off when someone knocked on the door. George: "Yes?"

A sweet feminine voice: "Are you okay, honey?"

"Sure." He went on drying.

She opened the door. It was a blond woman, thirtyish, slender and nice-looking in a wholesome way, wearing a moderately sexy black nightgown. She looked familiar. She said, "Can I come in?"

George wrapped the towel around himself, annoyed. "What if I say no?" Then he got it. She was the somewhat robotic wife from the movie *Allen*, which had come out around Christmas. He'd loved the movie—he'd seen it twice—about a man, Allen Barkley, raised in an artificial world who, unbeknownst to himself, was the star of a very popular TV show. Everyone in his world, including his wife, knew it was a sham. So this would be *George*. The wife's name on the show was Jenny. George couldn't remember her "real" name in the movie, or the name of the real-life actress who played her. She was one of those actresses you'd seen before but couldn't name. And here was the very same woman, as far as he could tell.

"Are you okay, George?"

"I'm okay. I needed a shower."

"You still hadn't come home when I went to bed. I was worried."

It suddenly hit George that he was, supposedly, being broadcast live to a world audience, and had been since he woke up. Millions, in theory, were watching him. Was that really happening? It was a little disorienting. He said, "What?"

"I was worried about you."

Now her previous remark registered. "I was out with Mike." Mike was Allen's best friend—George guessed his character had been out doing male bonding things with the man. If not, what did it matter?

Jenny made a face. "I'm not surprised. I wish you'd learn to say no to him once in a while."

George didn't want to have that conversation. "Yeah, well, I'm here now."

She smiled, a little suggestively. "Well, just dry off and come to bed. Okay, sweetie?" She moved in close and gave him a kiss, then said softly, "Okay?"

George smiled himself, understanding the situation. "Okay." He fought to keep from laughing.

She smiled again and drifted out, closing the door behind her. George held himself a little longer, then burst out laughing. He managed to muffle it a little, but Jenny could probably hear him. It didn't matter. In the movie, it'd been a while since they'd had sex. So she'd been trying to re-ignite their sex life. George, the moviegoer, had been attracted to her.

He finished drying off and wrapped the towel around his waist again. He found a razor and shaving cream in the cabinet above the sink and gave himself a much-needed shave. Then he went to the basement and threw his clothes in the dryer. Then he took the towel off—he didn't want to be wet from it when he got in bed with her. Should he feel guilty about having sex with her? No. He'd been forced to jump through too many hoops. He went upstairs, tossed the towel in the bathroom, and looked for her. Their bedroom was the second door he tried; the first had opened into a guest room with stuff stored in it.

He imagined Allen was the pajama type, but he decided to skip the pajamas for now. He hadn't worn any since he was a kid. The darkened room looked—as far as he could tell—'50s/modern, like the living room. He climbed into bed. Jenny, lying on her stomach, rolled to her side, and said, "Come here, darling." George did, and kissed her. It'd been months since he'd been with a woman. It was awkward with her at first, but it got better and better.

After they finished, she surprised him by hugging him. He returned the hug. Jenny: "That was wonderful, darling." She held him tight. Was he seeing some real affection? He hoped so. George: "You were wonderful." After a while they let go and shifted away from each other. George slept on his back, Jenny on her stomach, but with an arm across his chest. That was another pleasant surprise. As he was falling asleep, he wondered if he'd still be here when he woke up.

"Get up, George." She was shaking him. He opened his eyes—

morning light was in the room. He liked the room in daylight. She was wearing one towel around her body and another around her hair. "I've got some Café Roast coffee on—you need to take a shower."

"Okay." He rolled out of bed—he'd always been even worse than the average person at getting up. There was a digital clock on a nightstand by the bed; it was 7:02 a.m. He lumbered toward the bedroom door.

Jenny looked at him and laughed. "You forgot to put on pajamas."

He smiled. "Yeah. Uh, where was my head?" They probably blocked out the nakedness somehow.

She laughed again and left him. He went into the bathroom and took another shower, by the end of which he was pretty much awake. It occurred to him that it was strange that he was sleeping so much. His character had had good reason to be tired the night before, but George really hadn't. He wasn't sure how long it had been since he'd started all this, but it hadn't been that long, and he'd been unconscious several times already. He had just had sex, of course, but that by itself didn't explain it. Whatever. He didn't have answers. He dried off, wrapped the towel around himself, went back to the bedroom, found a comb, combed his hair, and went downstairs.

She was in the kitchen, dressed for business—she was a secretary—drinking coffee. As he passed her, she asked, "What are you doing?"

He didn't stop. "Getting my clothes."

She called to him as he went down the basement stairs. "They're in the dresser. Would you like me to pick some out for you?"

He called back, "That's okay." He pulled his clothes out of the dryer, got dressed, and put his wallet in his back pocket. He knew what Allen's clothes were like. He didn't want them on himself. He went back up to the kitchen.

Jenny: "You can't go to work like that!"

"I know. I need to do something." He didn't want to sit down and have a conversation with her—it would be uncomfortable. That meant he had to skip breakfast. He walked into the living room. "Have you seen my car keys?"

Jenny, in an affectionate, condescending tone: "*George*, they're on the dresser, where they always are."

"Thanks." He could eat on the road. He wasn't that hungry now—he never was so soon after getting up. He went upstairs to the bedroom and got the keys from the dresser. Regarding breakfast, he didn't like the idea of spending what little money he had, since presumably it had to last him until the end of all of this. Then it occurred to him that he could take whatever cash his character had on hand. It wasn't stealing—he was the character. And he'd have it in the next world. He heard her coming up the stairs. He opened the top dresser drawer—no cash.

She appeared in the doorway. "What do you have to do?"

"Oh . . . stuff." He tried the drawer of the nightstand—inside he found some bills, mostly ones, and took them. He started for the door.

Jenny: "What are you doing?"

George: "Getting some money."

"It's *our* money. I wish you'd ask. What do you need it for?"

He stopped. He'd thought the money belonged to his character. He counted it—$23. He put $12 back in the drawer. "I'll just take half."

"That's fine, but what do you need it for?" She was blocking the door.

"I need money." Putting the bills in his wallet, he tried to get around her.

"For what?" She was still blocking him.

He stood still. "Lunch and whatever. It's 11 bucks."

She stood aside. "Well, okay." He went through, and she followed him downstairs. "It's just you've been acting funny. I worry."

"I wish you wouldn't. I'll be okay." He reached the living room and kept moving, toward the front door.

"Honey?"

He turned. "Yes."

"Remember we're having dinner with Mike and Claire tonight."

He hated telling someone he'd be somewhere or do something and then not following through. If he couldn't follow through, that was one thing. If he just chose not to, that was breaking his word. If he knew when he gave his word that he probably wouldn't be able to do whatever it was, that was just as bad. And he didn't plan to be in town at dinnertime. "Uh . . . thanks for the reminder. I . . . uh . . . wasn't thinking about it."

"I wish you'd tell me where you're going."

He thought about what he should say. Then he wondered why he was dealing with this. She wasn't real. And if all this were real, she'd just be someone who was using him. Why was he playing this game? On the other hand, he'd just had sex with her. He said, "It's okay, darling."

"Aren't you forgetting something?"

He looked at her, puzzled. She pursed her lips. He smiled, then went over and gave her a big kiss.

She raised her eyebrows. "Boy!"

He smiled. "Boy. Goodbye, sweetheart."

"Goodbye, darling."

He left, closing the front door behind him. He didn't expect to see her again. The car, a new-looking silver Surad Focus, was in the driveway. He didn't own a car in real life, and hadn't driven in a while. An elderly Asian man next door waved and said, "Good morning, George!"

He waved backed. "Morning." He got in the car, started it, and backed out—fortunately, it was an automatic. Then he put it in drive and went. Of course, he still needed to decide where to go. In a way, it'd be the perfect rebellion to hang around Ocean Breeze, instead of trying to escape as Allen had. But he just couldn't resist trying to leave. Even if that was what his real handlers wanted, he was going to do it.

With some difficulty, he got the radio on. It was tuned to a jazz station—Allen liked jazz. George hit the scan button and stopped on a '70s rock song. He wondered what the Allen handlers were thinking. He imagined they were moderately worried right now, trying to figure out his intentions. Unlike the Allen world in the movie, the worlds George had been in had been right in every detail as far as he could tell. If one included the mistakes and limitations of the people who ran the show as part of this world, this one was exactly right as well.

He came up with a plan that was insolently simple—he would drive right to the limits of the program's world, if they let him. If they didn't he would improvise. He didn't know his way around, but that wouldn't be a big problem—Ocean Breeze was small. The weather was pleasant, of course—he drove with the windows down. It was sunny, with lots of blue sky and a few puffy clouds. In that it was similar to the Xerxi world, but he knew it wasn't real, even in the context of this world, and it was much less appealing. The town had a '50s/modern look—spotless streets, relatively small but attractive houses—not too similar, not too different—nicely mowed lawns. The streets were arranged in a regular, orderly way, unlike the streets of Sawyerville and Unionville. This place was supposed to epitomize suburbia. Unionville was a real suburb, and they had little in common.

He considered breakfast, and decided to skip it. He still wasn't hungry, and he was excited by the idea of beating the Allen handlers and escaping. He drove as far as he could in one direction, hit a T-intersection, turned right and again drove as far as he could. This brought him to a cul-de-sac; he turned in it and went the other way. This took him to within sight of the beach. Now he knew where the ocean was. He needed to get to the other side of town. He turned left, drove a few blocks, and turned left again. He thought about driving through the nice business district, just to check it out, but decided to let it go. He drove several blocks on this road and hit another cul-de-sac. The Allen handlers would assume he knew the town backwards and forwards. What would they make of his driving? Well, that was their problem. He drove back out of the cul-de-sac street and took a left. The next left would have taken him to yet another cul-de-sac—were the real handlers mocking him?—but then he hit an intersection with a more important-looking road, though still only a two-laner. Now he turned left, and soon he was fairly sure this would take him right off the island, if the Allen handlers let him go. The station had played a series of '70s-ish rock songs, which was fine. The traffic slowed down; then it stopped completely. Well, it wasn't a surprise. He leaned back and waited. Most of the cars looked new. None were junkers. Most were mid-sized or smaller. The progress was stop and go for several songs, then it got even slower, more stop than go. He kept waiting. They never tried to cut off his progress completely, but the car's advances got steadily smaller and steadily less frequent. After maybe 45 minutes he pulled over, shifted to park, got out—leaving the car running, and leaving the windows down—and started walking. He assumed he was parked illegally.

He'd walked maybe 200 yards when the cars began to speed up; in less than a minute they were going at normal speed. George considered his options, then said, "I'll bite," and headed back to his car. When he got there a police car was parked behind it. The cop got out; it was Sullok.

George walked up to him. Sullok met him between their cars and said, smiling: "George, what are you doing? You know you can't park here." The uniform looked good on him. He had his hair in a ponytail, which looked a bit odd with his uniform hat.

George looked into his eyes—which he tended not to do with people—and said, "I want to go home." Then he turned and walked to his car.

"What's wrong?" George kept walking. He didn't have anything else to say. He got in his car.

Sullok walked after him, and said, his tone no longer friendly, "George, you stay there." George pulled out into an opening in the traffic, which was no longer heavy. He hadn't turned off the radio. He occasionally glanced in the rearview mirror. Sullok returned to his car, hit the lights and siren, and came after him. The other cars pulled over; Sullok was soon behind him. If he continued, he'd be giving both sets of handlers an excuse to keep him here, by putting him in jail. He had assumed the real handlers wanted to see him escape, but he didn't know what they wanted. He pulled over, and turned off the car. Sullok followed suit, then got out and walked briskly to George's car.

Sullok leaned over and stuck his head in the window; his face was angry—he was in character. "*What* is the matter with you? *What* are you doing?"

George wanted to make sarcastic remarks—which would be easy, given the circumstances—but that was what they wanted him to do. Or maybe it wasn't, but in any event he wasn't going that route. He looked at Sullok, and said: "I've said what I have to say to you. From now on I'll just play this role."

Sullok straightened up, clenched and unclenched his jaw, shook his head, and then paced once, briefly, back and forth. Then: "I have no idea what you just said to me!"

George turned off the radio. "Never mind. Go ahead."

Sullok was still acting exasperated. " 'Go ahead.' You pulled over, walked away from your car for no reason—and you left it running—you walked back, drove away when you knew I needed to talk to you, and now you're talking gibberish."

"I think you should give me a ticket."

Sullok, cooling down: "I could take you in. Do you know that?"

"Yes." He took a deep breath. "Is that going to be necessary?"

Sullok was mostly calmed down. "Ordinarily it wouldn't be. But I don't know, the way you're acting . . . ."

Were the Allen handlers in contact with him? Probably. Not that he needed them. George said, "I think I can act okay from here on in."

"Well . . . ."

Suddenly George felt like he'd been sucking up to the guy. His face hardened and he looked away, out the front window.

Sullok: "Now what?"

"Nothing. Do what you want to do."

"Well, if that's your attitude . . . wait here." He walked back to his car. George turned the key halfway so he could listen to the radio, and wondered what would happen. He watched the traffic. If the guy took too long, he'd pull out and make a run for it, even though they'd surely get him. After a couple of minutes Sullok returned, carrying a ticket. George turned the key to cut off the radio. Sullok handed him the ticket and said: "That's for stopping on the highway. Driving off like that, that just never happened." He paused for effect. "*Because* it's you. If I didn't like you, George, you'd be on your way to jail. Okay?"

George hesitated. He didn't want to be nice to the guy. "I understand."

Sullok, friendly tone: "Anyway, shouldn't you be at work?"

"Personal holiday."

"Personal holiday? What for?"

George shrugged. "Sometimes a guy just needs a personal holiday."

Sullok nodded, playing the part of a man pretending to understand. "I know what ya mean. Say, you seen Mike lately?"

This was quite a chat to be having on the side of a state highway. George supposed the Allen handlers were trying to give him second thoughts about whatever he had planned. "Last night."

"How's he doin'?"

George shrugged. "Fine."

Sullok nodded. "Okay. Good. Well, take it easy out there, okay?"

"You got it." Sullok started to walk off, looked back and waved. George waved back. Then he started the car again, pulled onto the road, and drove. Sullok pulled out not far behind him. That wouldn't be good if they trapped George behind a traffic jam again—he couldn't pull over and walk like he had before. He turned left off the highway at the first side road, drove a little way, turned left again, drove to a dead end, turned around, and drove back to the highway. Sullok's car was nowhere in sight. And George couldn't have that far to go now before he got to the bridge.

The traffic started to get heavier. Then the car in front of him slowed down, more than the traffic required. It wasn't a traffic jam, yet; George was just behind a slow driver. He decided to let it go, for a while anyway. Then the guy slowed down even more. There was too much oncoming traffic for George to try to pass. He gave the guy a long honk. There was no response. Then they were both trapped behind an even slower driver. Then they were all in a traffic jam. Traffic was stop and go, then mostly stop. George saw the guy in front of him, a young guy, glance into his rearview mirror apprehensively. George was their livelihood, and he might be trying to escape. Then the traffic was completely stopped. Now, at least, he could see the bridge. The oncoming traffic thinned out. A few people did U-turns and drove back toward town. This provided him with his only advances for several songs. He knew the Allen handlers could wait as long as he could. That thought made him wonder what they would do if he stayed here for hours, or even overnight. He imagined sooner or later they would do something—maybe have a cop tell everyone that they had determined that the bridge was unsafe and closed it. Actually, now that he thought about it, that's what he would do if he was in their shoes. In any event he wasn't going to wait. He did a U-turn himself, drove to the first side street, turned right onto it, drove a bit, and parked on the side of the road. He didn't want to give them an excuse to arrest him. He rolled up the windows, turned off the car, got out, locked the door, put the keys in his pocket, and started walking back to the highway.

He reached the highway, crossed it, and walked toward the bridge. He was halfway there when the traffic cleared again. This time he didn't go back. A car pulled over just in front of him. The driver's door opened; the driver got out and turned to face him. The guy was middle-aged and wore a baseball cap. He said, "George, what are you doing here?"

George was friendly: "Walking." He didn't stop.

"Out here?"

George looked over his shoulder, still moving. "Yeah."

The guy had to raise his voice: "Well, need a lift?"

Still looking over his shoulder: "No, thanks." Then he turned his head back toward the bridge.

Now the guy had to yell: "You sure?"

George yelled back: "Yes." Soon after that the guy drove past him, waving as he did. George returned the wave.

Not long after that he was at the bridge, which was not closed. Furthermore, due to bad planning on the part of the Allen handlers, it had a footpath. This meant they couldn't arrest him for walking across it. He started to do so. He sang a few lines of the last song he'd heard, "I'm For You," by the Ice Men. A few cars honked, and a driver yelled, "What the hell are you doin'?" as if he was doing something outrageous. His path was two feet wide, with handrails. He couldn't be safer, and he had a great view of the water. He reached the other side and kept walking, and didn't look back.

The highway would take him to a chemical plant. In the movie they turned Allen back at the plant by saying there was a leak. They'd do the same to George if he followed the highway. So he crossed it again and walked away from it. A forest began not far from the road—he entered it. Somebody else honked, as if a man walking into a forest was unheard of. Then he heard a familiar voice yell, "George, where are you going?" He just kept walking. The forest seemed real enough—the trees were varied, and there was underbrush. In fact it was a bit difficult to walk it, but he'd make do. The voice yelled again: "George! It's me, Mike!"

George looked over his shoulder. It was Allen's buddy in the movie, running up to him. George hated to stop moving, but he'd feel like a jerk if he didn't. He stopped and turned. "Hi, Mike." The guy had parked his cab on the side of the highway. George: "Hey, man, don't leave your car there. I just got ticketed for that."

"Hell with that." Mike stopped next to George and caught his breath, hands on his hips.

George: "What are you doing out here?"

Mike laughed. "What am I—what about you? I'm working."

George looked in the cab—it was empty. "There's nobody in your cab."

Mike: "Yeah, I gotta pick somebody up at Purity. Hey—come with me." Purity was the chemical plant.

George pretended to think it over. "Pass. I'm gonna go commune with nature. You know I never walked in these woods in my life."

"Me neither.... You oughta go the other way, anyway." He pointed in the opposite direction. "You get a nice view of Ocean Breeze." He was right—at the edge of the woods was a narrow strip of beach, then the water, then the town. George had seen it as he crossed the bridge. But the way he was headed would take him to the dome much sooner. Mike added, "And I think this is private property."

George shrugged. "I'll take my chances."

Pause. "Well, I guess you can do what you want. I, uh, I needed to talk to you about somethin'."

"Uh . . . call the house later."

Pause. "Okay, well, I'll talk to you later."

"Sounds good. Take care."

"Bye." Mike turned and headed back to his cab. George resumed his walk. He angled over to near the edge of the woods, from which he could see the water and, if he looked over his shoulder, the bridge and a bad view of the town. He hadn't promised he would be at his house when Mike called. He'd implied it, but he wouldn't feel bound to that after he formally discovered the dome and understood Mike had been lying to him for years. That led him to the thought that he already knew about the dome and knew Mike had been lying—he was playing a pointless game. Beyond that, he was from a different reality that Mike, probably, knew nothing about. In that sense he was deceiving Mike. He was a kind of double agent who, nevertheless, answered to no one.

He kept walking. After a while he could see the dome. Of course, he could see it anytime he was "outdoors" here, just by looking up. But now it looked less real. Or perhaps it was just that he knew what it was—maybe he wouldn't have noticed anything unusual if he hadn't. He was relatively close, he was sure, and moving at a decent pace despite the underbrush. There were no roads visible, except the highway, which was steadily becoming more remote. They hadn't wanted roads out here, for obvious reasons. In spite of everything, he figured they'd get someone out to him before he reached the dome. They could tell him he was trespassing.

He saw a boat in the distance, near the town, headed his way. That'd be the easiest way to reach him, so, reluctantly, he angled away from the shoreline. He looked back occasionally—after a while he couldn't see the water. At that point he tried to go straight toward the dome. He had no way of knowing if he was going straight, however, now that the shore was gone. He sighted a particular tree straight in front of him, as far away as he could see, then walked to it, then spotted another tree, walked to that, and kept going using that system. It was a way to avoid getting turned around, but the forest was so dense now that moving forward wasn't easy. The dome wasn't much help. However, it did look different in front of him than behind him—he was sure of that much.

The more he saw of the forest the more it impressed him. It seemed just as real here as by the highway; he even saw a few squirrels. Nevertheless, he doubted there would be many cameras out here. The handlers would be dealing with lots of long and/or strange shots. He guessed they'd had him on screen pretty much the whole time though. He imagined a network of rotating cameras that could cover him anywhere in the forest, except maybe when he got behind the odd tree. He sure hadn't seen a camera though, here or anywhere else.

Maybe 20 minutes after he'd left Mike he heard a gravelly male voice call out: "You there!"

He looked around, not stopping, and saw, to his surprise, an older man, needing a shave, wearing overalls, no shirt, and carrying a shotgun.

Ocean Breeze was supposed to be on an island off the California coast—this guy didn't look like California. George stopped walking. "Yes?"

The man approached him. His tone became less hostile. "This is my land. What are you doin' on it?"

"Taking a walk."

The man was shocked. "Here?! Well . . . never mind. I can let it go, but you just turn around and go back the way you come."

George: "Uh-huh. . . . Say, how much land do you own out here?"

The man became quite angry. "Never you mind! That's my business! Now git!"

George: " 'Git.' Yeah. Well you know what? Fuck you. In a manner of speaking this is my forest. It sure isn't yours. You're just an actor."

Man, waving shotgun: "What the hell are you talkin' about? You done lost your *mind*, son! Now you better git!"

"Can they hear me? I hope they can hear me out here in the woods. Here's my message: I hope the viewers stop buying the products advertised on this show. If they can't hear that now they'll hear it later."

Pause, then in a changed tone: "Look, what do you want?"

"I want you to leave."

"Leave? This is my property!"

"I tell you what. If you apologize to me, and walk away now, and I don't see anyone else until I leave the dome, I won't go after you people. . . ."

Man, angry: "What the . . . ?"

"Shut up. One more word out of you and I'm gonna see to it that whoever's running this goes broke." Presumably someone was in contact with the actor. They wouldn't let him play this by ear. George paused; the man was silent, though he looked furious. "I'll tear into the sponsors here, and as soon as I'm out I'll rip into them to whoever will listen. I'll also rip all of this and everybody involved in it, and I'll sue. And if I can think of another way to stick it to all of you I will. Now, I want to find the wall myself; that's why I went to all this trouble. That's why I played along with whoever's really running this. You don't know anything about that. So what I want is just say you're sorry—and as far as I'm concerned you're apologizing on behalf of whoever's running this—and everybody leaves me alone. Your move."

The furious look was gone; there was now a look of professional disdain. In a very different voice, one that included the disdain, he said, "Okay, yeah, sorry." With that he tossed the gun aside and walked off; even his walk was different now.

George laughed and resumed walking. He'd won. Remembering his car keys, he took them out of his pocket and dropped them on the ground. Nevertheless, he still had to proceed by spotting a tree and walking to it, then repeating, which was even more of a pain now. But soon he could see the dome clearly enough to use it to guide himself. He sang as much of "I'm for You" as he knew. The dome became more and more clear, then he could spot it right in front of him between the trees. It was somewhat anti-climactic when he actually reached it. Unlike Allen, he'd learned nothing he didn't already know for sure. He'd merely beaten the handlers at a game. And not even the real handlers.

There was a path along the wall, paved. He followed it. The view was interesting, if a little disconcerting. The dome—an arm's length away—stretched, curving, above him, and the curving path went as far as he could see in either direction. He could see the water again now, if he looked back. To his right, a few feet away, was a believable, dense forest.

After perhaps 15 minutes of walking, still in the forest, he reached a door. What would he do if it was locked? But that would serve no purpose for the Allen handlers. Once he was here, the jig would be up. The door had a handle rather than a knob. He turned down the handle and pushed the door forward, then stepped through the doorway and kept walking.

He was outside. There were people around him, heading his way, talking. A street went around the dome; other streets came off of the dome street like spokes. There were multi-story buildings and parking lots. There were lots of cars parked on the street in his immediate vicinity. Everything looked good, as far as George could see—it was an attractive, well-kept area, with mowed grassy strips and neat little trees around. He headed for one of the spoke streets. The people converged on him. A young woman placed herself in front of him, offering her hand: "George, it's an honor to meet you."

He shook her hand and said, "Thank you." He kept walking. These people varied greatly from one another, and they were not dressed '50s/modern. But they also weren't like real people—they were comedy movie crowd extras. They had to be fans who'd come to meet him. He was in a swarm, now, but he could still move forward. Everyone spoke at once. People asked for autographs, which he refused, as politely as he could. There appeared to be no one from the program here. But he'd be hearing from them eventually, if he stayed in this world.

Somebody said, "Hey, people, give him some space, okay?"

George: "Yes, thank you."

They backed off a little bit, temporarily, but soon it was as bad as before. He heard things like, "I watch you every day," "How did you know?", and "I've watched you since the beginning."

When were the real handlers going to take him out of this world? But he was playing their game to even think that. He was a celebrity here, and could live easy until they took him away. He'd just do his thing. He stopped walking. "People, could I have your attention, please?" They quieted down. They were all around him. "Thank you for coming.... I'm glad you liked the show, but it wasn't my show, and nobody asked me. I appreciate you coming, but I really need some down time. I'd like to be alone, if that's okay." He resumed walking. They all stood still for a moment. Then many of them said things to him. Then many, not necessarily the same ones, gradually converged on him again.

This time he ignored them. He'd rarely felt sorry for celebrities who complained about all the attention they got. Most of them sought attention, and they tended to want to have it both ways, to be able to turn the attention off and on like a faucet. But this was a little different. He hadn't volunteered, and he wasn't experiencing many of the benefits of fame. They were all around him, talking, pressing against him. He couldn't really ignore them, but he pretended to. Occasionally, one of them utterly blocked his path, and he had to go around the person, sometimes pushing his way around.

He heard a loud "thump." He heard expressions of surprise from the crowd, and suddenly he was getting a lot less attention. They were paying attention to the place the sound had come from. He was still getting more attention than he wanted, but the situation was more tolerable. He was curious, though; he worked his way through the crowd to the source of the thump. Now his fame did help him—people had been reluctant to leave him alone, but they were quick to get out of his way. Soon he could see the object of their attention, a wooden door in a door frame, standing by itself in the middle of the street. "Too much," he said. He assumed this was his ticket out.

People touched it, walked around it, tried and failed to open it. He didn't bother walking around it. "Mind if I try?" he asked a teenaged girl trying the knob. She stood aside, nodded pleasantly, and gestured toward the door with an upturned hand. He stepped up, turned the knob, and pulled the door open.

Across the threshold was a sumptuously furnished room, maybe a hotel room. There was a huge bed. The crowd reacted again, more or less like before. He shrugged and walked in.

# CHAPTER 8

George turned and looked back. The door was gone. The room, a bedroom, was big and plush. Light blue dominated. The carpet was thick. There was a chandelier, a desk, a chest of drawers, and assorted unnecessary tables and chairs. There were paintings, mirrors, vases of flowers, and various knick-knacks, including a glass egg. Through large, elegant windows he could see it was night. Where was he?

A lovely, dark-haired woman came in, wearing complicated red lingerie, a red sheer robe, and heels. "Enjoying yourself, Mr. Preston?" She had a vaguely European accent. She carried a fluted glass with something bubbling in it in one hand and a greenish bottle in the other.

"Sure."

She laughed. "Care for a little champagne?"

He answered, "If you insist." She laughed again. He frowned—he had a feeling he'd been in character. That wouldn't last.

She walked over, topping off the glass, and handed it to him. Then she took another glass out of the pocket of her robe and filled it. "I like you in these . . . blue jeans. Very American. Well . . . to us."

"Cheers." They clinked glasses. He had a passing thought that the champagne might be poisonous—he hadn't seen her fill his glass. Then he thought, so what? He shrugged and drank, quickly emptying his glass.

"George!" she said in surprise, as if he had done something interesting.

He stuck out his glass. "Please." Now she shrugged, and filled the glass again. He took a sip, and said, "Ah. . . . Listen, are you hungry?"

"Well," she said mischievously, "yes and no."

"Okay . . . well, I think I'd like something. How 'bout some caviar?"

"I love caviar!"

"Great." He looked around for a phone, saw one on the desk, and walked over to it. "What else?"

She was thrown off by this. "Well . . . what are you having?"

He sat at the desk, in an elegant wooden chair with a light blue cushion seat. "I don't know. They have a menu?"

She walked toward him, confused now. "I . . . I don't know. I didn't know we were coming up here to eat." She sat near him, at the edge of the bed. "I'm sure they can get you whatever you want."

"Okay. What's the number?"

She cleared her throat. Her tone was a bit cold now: "Just pick it up and ask for room service."

"Great," he said in a cheerful voice. He did as she'd suggested. The phone was in a very old-fashioned style—you spoke into a horn—and was as attractive as everything else.

A rich voice, with a bit of a French accent, said, "May we help you, sir?"

"Sure. I'd like some caviar . . . ."

"I see. And what kind of caviar would you like, sir?"

"Uh . . . what do you recommend?"

There was a brief silence. "Count Korikov is excellent."

"Okay. Some of that. Plenty for two."

"Very well, sir."

"And . . . ." What did he want? Steak? Italian? Chinese? He didn't want to order a cheeseburger or something just to thumb his nose at the handlers. "How about escargot?" He'd been hearing about that all his life—it'd be fun to try it.

"Very well."

"Is that an entrée?"

"Sir?"

"Is escargot an entrée?"

"It . . . can be. Would you like it that way, sir?"

"No. Make it an appetizer. As an entrée, something French." He happened to be looking at her. Her eyes widened.

The guy on the other end of the line: "I . . . see. Did you have anything particular in mind?"

"Not really. Can you recommend something?"

The guy was getting over his surprise now. "Just a moment, sir. Something appropriate. Perhaps bacon-and-leek quiche?"

"Sounds good. Hang on." He held the phone against his shoulder. "What do you want besides caviar?"

She gave him a nervous smile, then looked around. Her voice was rather weak. "I . . . I don't know. Perhaps I should leave."

"What's wrong?"

Nervous, confused, disappointed: "I . . . I don't understand what you're doing, Mr. Preston. This is no time to eat."

He looked directly at her. "I'm going to eat. I'm hungry. I don't want to put on a show. You're welcome to stay. What would you like to do?"

"Are you angry with me, Mr. Preston?"

"Why don't you call me George?"

"George. Are you angry with me?"

He thought it over. "I guess not. But I'd like to eat. If that's not okay, well, that's too bad. I hope you stay and eat with me, or just hang out if you don't want to eat. I just don't want to perform for you."

She thought about this. "I'll stay. I'll have some oysters on the half-shell." She added mischievously, "Maybe later you perform."

He smiled. He liked to meet the world halfway, though it often failed to work. He put the phone back against his ear. "Still there?"

Slightly annoyed: "Of course, sir."

"Thanks for holding. Throw in some oysters on the half-shell."

"Of course. Will that be all, sir?"

"Hang on." He put the phone on his shoulder again. "What would you like to drink?"

At this she brightened. "More champagne. Almagnal, if they have it."

"Champagne. Do you have Almagnal?"

"Of course, sir."

"Bottle of that. I guess that's got it."

"Very well, sir."

George hung up. He asked his companion: "Any idea how long that'll take?"

The question surprised her. "I wasn't thinking about it . . . . Fifteen, twenty minutes. You've . . . used room service before, haven't you?"

"Not like this."

She laughed. "Come now, Mr. . . . George. You are no stranger to all of this."

He smiled. No point in arguing with her. She was okay—she was probably a better person than his "wife" in the last world. Now how to put in the time till the food got there. It was an awkward length of time for the situation. Which, it occurred to him, meant she had been right in the first place that they shouldn't order anything. He got up and sat next to her on the bed. It had a thick, light blue coverlet over it—even the coverlet looked extremely expensive. She smiled as he sat down. He said: "Tell me about yourself. We've got some time."

She looked away, her eyes half-closed, and said, demurely, "There's . . . not much to tell."

He said, "Hmm." Then he gave her a small smile, and slowly leaned toward her. He wasn't too good at this, but he was giving it his best shot. He kissed her. She made an "mmm" sound. He put his arms around her, slowly; she did the same. He held her tight, kissing her. Then after a while they were lying side by side on the bed. He thought, at this inappropriate time, that he still had little idea what this world was. He was some sort of rich playboy, but that didn't tell him much. His character had met this woman recently, for what that was worth. She obviously expected him to go further than he was going, but didn't say anything about it. She gave him an "Oh, George!" a couple of times.

Of course, by the time the room buzzer rang, he didn't want to stop. But it'd be rude to ignore whoever had brought their food, and she wasn't going anywhere. He pulled away, sitting up, and gently squeezed her shoulder. "I think it's time to eat."

She sighed. "We don't have to eat."

"I know. But I don't want to leave the guy out there. We've got a lot of time."

She made a small frown, still lying on her side. "You're very sweet, George. You're... not what I expected."

He liked that. "Thank you." The buzzer sounded again. He followed the sound to a relatively small room adjoining the bedroom, just as sumptuous despite its limited space. He looked through the eyehole in the door. There, wearing a waiter's uniform, blond hair in a ponytail, was Sullok. He stood behind a room service cart.

George considered for a moment. Then he said, "Go away," and returned to the bedroom. His companion was still lying down. "Miss me?" he asked.

She smiled. "Oh, yes."

He heard a loud "Crack!" behind him, walked back toward the front room and saw a steel fist withdrawing from a hole it had just made in the door. That was a surprise. George cleared his throat. "I said, 'Go away.'" The fist came through the door again, with another loud "Crack!" Then it went to the doorknob—the whole forearm was steel—and opened the door.

George nodded. "John Thorpe." This wasn't any particular John Thorpe movie, but could have been any from the late '70s or early '80s.

He heard her running up beside him. "George!"

Sullok wheeled in the cart. His face had no expression. George said, "What the fuck," and ran toward him. Sullok was lifting a metal cover on the cart, revealing black, shining nunchucks. George easily ran around the cart and hit Sullok on the chin with his right fist. This knocked Sullok back; the cart fell over.

George moved forward and tried to hit Sullok with his left, but Sullok—impressively, given his height—managed to duck under it. Sullok then hit George in the ribs with a left. The right was the steel hand, but the blow was painful, all the same, and threw George off-balance. Sullok then dove for the nunchucks. George jumped on top of him. The woman yelled George's name again. Sullok grabbed the weapon with his steel hand. George, straddling Sullok, grabbed the hand. Then he got a better idea. He picked up the gleaming metal cover, reassuringly heavy, and slammed it into Sullok's head, producing a crashing sound. He raised the cover—Sullok now had a gash on the back of his head—and Sullok rolled to his side, swinging the nunchucks and knocking George off with them.

George fell to his side and quickly scrambled up. Sullok faced him, a couple of paces away, breathing heavily. Of course Sullok would have been better off just hitting George with his steel hand, but no matter. Sullok's face was still expressionless. Furthermore, he had not yet uttered a word, which wasn't like him. It took most of the satisfaction out of not talking to him. George said, deadpan, "No, Mr. Sullok, I expect you to die."

Sullok's face didn't react, but he came forward. George did the same. Sullok swung the nunchucks, high; George ducked under them and continued forward, head-butting the guy. George tried to tackle him; he rolled to George's left. George tried to roll with him and felt the nunchucks slam into his head. This brought George to his knees; he hopped to the left, successfully avoiding Sullok, and got back to a fighting stance.

Sullok rushed him again; he stepped back and to the left, avoiding him. Where were Thorpe's guns? Still avoiding Sullok, he jumped over the overturned cart; as he did he noticed the cover. It had worked pretty well before. He quickly bent, grabbed it by the handle with both hands, and brought it up in time to block the nunchucks. Crashing sound. He and Sullok faced each other again. Sullok came forward, again swinging the nunchucks high. George blocked with the cover and then slammed it into Sullok's face. Another crash. Sullok staggered backwards.

"That's enough, Mr. Preston." The woman was standing beside him, pointing a small gun at his head.

He sighed and dropped the heavy cover. His arms felt better. He frowned. It didn't make much difference, really. He tried to think of a wisecrack, then stopped—that'd be playing their game. He'd kind of liked the sport of the fight with Sullok. Then he was suddenly curious about something. He asked her, "What's your name?"

She smiled. "I told you, Mr. Preston. Lacey Delight."

"Oh." He smiled. He went ahead with a wisecrack, anyway: "Seven deadly sins. No waiting." Sullok was standing directly in front of him now, looking mildly annoyed. He hit George in the jaw with his steel fist, and George was out.

He woke up in another large, nicely furnished room—this one had a lot of dark wood and a lot of books. He was lying on a very comfortable couch; he wore handcuffs. Sullok was here, wearing what looked like black silk pajamas. There was also a bald, middle-aged man with a wide build wearing a monocle and a gray uniform. This man sat in an elegant armchair facing the couch, a couple of yards away. Lacey Delight, unfortunately, was not here. The new man would be the main villain. His comic-book appearance was more late-'70s Thorpe movie than early-'80s. Noticing George was awake, the man smiled and set down the book he'd been reading. From where George was, he could make out the title—*An Empire Falls*, by the Russian novelist Fyodor Tulginsky. Cheerfully, the man said: "Ah, Mr. Preston. I see you have awakened. Dr. Maxim, at your service." He smiled confidently and nodded. The accent was, inappropriately, British.

How should George play this? He sat up. The handcuffs were attached to a chain that ran to a ring on a metal plate bolted to the floor. He looked at Sullok, who was, as usual in this world, expressionless. He was tempted to make a sarcastic remark about that, but kept quiet.

Maxim: "How are you feeling, Mr. Preston?"

Now that he mentioned it, George's jaw was sore. He moved it back and forth. A remark came to him to the effect that he wondered how many times he was going to hear "Mr. Preston" before this was through, but he let it go.

"Not feeling talkative, Mr. Preston?" Maxim gave a small laugh.

Sullok certainly wasn't talkative. Were they getting even with George for blowing him off earlier? Whatever—George would follow suit. Let Maxim carry the story. George was taking a break.

Maxim's voice picked up an edge. "You're hurting my feelings, XZ."

George breathed deeply in and out, watching Maxim.

Maxim now produced a childly, pouty tone: "Don't you have anything to say to me?"

George smiled.

Maxim smiled. "But I'm being a bad host. Can I offer you a drink?"

George looked him over. Maxim's shirt buttoned up the left front, to an inch-high collar that didn't fold forward, like an ordinary collar does. A thin silver line connected the monocle to the collar. The guy's eyebrows were white.

"Iron Fist, please inquire as to whether our friend would care for a drink?" Sullok walked toward George, making a fist with his non-steel hand.

George stood up. When Sullok was close enough George tried to kick his left knee. Sullok jerked his leg aside—the kick connected but had little effect—and swung his fist at George's nose. George rolled his head but caught it on his cheekbone. He almost fell, but didn't. He shook his head and blinked, and said: "I don't like your game, asshole. I want to go home." He was immediately frustrated with himself for saying anything.

Maxim beamed. "Ah, we have a conversation. I'm afraid I can't allow you to leave, but how about that drink?"

George said, angrily, "How about you undo the cuffs and we fight like men?"

"We did, my good man, and you lost. Perhaps we didn't follow gentlemen's rules, entirely, but I don't believe you did either." He paused. "Nevertheless, you amuse me, sir."

George was humorless. "It's not mutual."

Maxim's smile disappeared. "I see. Perhaps, then, we should dispense with the pleasantries."

George stared at Sullok, then at Maxim, and said coldly, "Please."

"Very well. I know you've been trying very hard to locate my humble home. But it'd have done you little good, anyway, after tonight. My operation has reached a point at which I'll need to relocate to a rather more private place. An island in the Pacific, not far from Hawaii, as it happens. I've spent some time preparing it. I should be able to manage my affairs quite nicely there. A shame you'll never see it." He paused for effect. "From there I'll be able to monitor the infection of all the world's computer systems with my virus—splendid thing, no chance they'll cure it, without me. But I'll sell my cure." He chuckled. "I'll sell it again and again. It's a disk, you see—the purchaser inserts it in his system; it kills the virus, but it renders itself inoperable after one use. And, unfortunately, my price will be a bit steep. By the way, I've got my system for receiving payments and delivering disks in lovely shape." He smiled. "My home here isn't safe though, you see, not anymore—as I said, not enough privacy." He pronounced "privacy" with a short i. "So it will have to burn down. I'm afraid you, my dear friend, must suffer the same fate." He turned to Sullok, said "Iron Fist," and clapped his hands smartly. Sullok left the room.

Maxim's scheme definitely moved the story out of the '70s; it sounded too computer-oriented even for the early '80s. And it sounded weak for a Thorpe villain scheme, even though it would be terrible if it happened in the real world. Whatever; George had more immediate concerns. He asked: "How do you know I won't get away?" Even asking that was a kind of cliché, from spy movie spoofs, but screw it.

Maxim's expression hardened. "How?"

George shrugged. Sullok returned with several orange plastic gallon containers. He opened one and began to splash its contents around the room. Soon George could smell gasoline.

George, ignoring Maxim, began to search himself for gadgets.

"Looking for something, Mr. Preston? Perhaps a cigarette?"

Fuck you, George thought. He found nothing, of course. Sullok worked quickly. Maxim kept the silences from getting too long with, "You're sure you won't have that drink," and later, "I hope there are no hard feelings."

George looked around for a possible means of escape, and saw nothing. He was playing their game, but he was willing to do so to avoid being burned alive. The handlers were playing awfully rough. Nevertheless he didn't feel nervous. It was all too unreal.

Sullok finished and looked inquiringly at Maxim. Maxim waved him through a doorway and followed him there. Standing in the doorway, Maxim said: "Forgive the smell, Mr. Preston. I know it's a bit high." He drew a silver lighter from his pocket and flicked it on. Bowing, he said, "Adieu, XZ." Then he dropped the lighter on the carpet and withdrew. Fire spread rapidly around the room.

The sight of the flames got to George—suddenly he was scared. He knew he would soon panic. He looked around the room again—nothing to help him. He pulled hard on his handcuffs. They were strong enough. He examined the plate bolted to the floor and the bolts themselves—they were sound. The flames were all over the room, and he had to keep his head low to avoid inhaling the smoke. He realized what he'd have to do. He'd have to stand up and take deep breaths until the smoke knocked him out or killed him. He hated the idea, but it was better than burning alive. He stood up. Then he heard someone coming, running. He squatted and got his head close to the floor.

"George!" It was Lacey Delight, in the doorway.

"Over here! I'm handcuffed to the floor!"

"I've got the key!"

"Keep your head down and hurry!" He felt a sting of guilt—maybe the right thing would have been to tell her to stay out. But then again, if he died what would happen to her? And screw it, anyway—he wasn't a white knight.

She bent so her head was at waist level, ran over to him, dropped to the floor, and unlocked the handcuffs. They ran out, heads low. Through the doorway was a hall; the flames were much less intense. She said, "This way," took his hand, and pulled him forward.

He took his hand away, so they could move faster. "I'm right behind you. Thanks for saving my life."

"It was my pleasure." At the end of the hall were carpeted stairs; at the top of the stairs was a large kitchen—the flames had barely begun here. The two of them ran through the kitchen, her leading, then through a doorway to a nicely furnished porch. It was still night. There was no fire here, but they kept running, opening a screen door to get to a patio with plastic furniture and a swimming pool, all surrounded by a stone wall. He followed her through an archway to a car, a purple RCP. She said, quickly: "Get in. I'll drive."

"You got it." He pulled open the door and jumped in. The interior was black; it had a new car smell. She got in, fumbled for her keys, and started it. "Lacey." She looked at him. He quickly kissed her on the mouth. "Thank you for saving my life."

She smiled warmly. "Like I told you, darling, it was my pleasure." She stroked his cheek where Sullok had hit him. "My poor darling."

"I'll be okay. We better go."

She nodded and turned away, then shifted into first and drove. They went down a long driveway, through a well-kept estate like you'd see in a movie about British aristocrats.

He was quiet for a while, watching the scenery. They drove through an open gateway out of the estate. Beyond was a country road curving along steep hillsides. She accelerated. He glanced at the speedometer—they were soon doing 65. Much too fast for a road like this in reality, no problem in a Thorpe movie. It crossed his mind that they wouldn't have just left her behind. They would have taken her with them, or, if they were double-crossing her for some reason, killed her. If he asked her about it, there would be some sort of explanation, but it wouldn't really make sense. He didn't say anything. It was a problem with the story, not with her. He trusted her.

She said playfully, "Cat got your tongue, George?"

"Not exactly. I'm wondering what our next move is."

She laughed. "I'm not a spy, but perhaps you should report in."

"Good idea. I'm wondering what to do about you."

She didn't like that. "What do you mean?"

"You're in great danger." She was a bad woman who'd turned good, and this was the middle of the film. She almost certainly wasn't the main love interest. The story would want to kill her off.

"Well, aren't you too?"

"Uh, yes and no." Maybe if he got her to go far away she'd be okay. A character like her wouldn't necessarily have to be near Thorpe when she died, but if she just checked herself out of the movie completely she might become so irrelevant there'd be no dramatic point in killing her. He couldn't see a Thorpe girl flying to another continent and then being murdered by order of the main villain. A killing like that would seem empty to viewers. "Well, let's not worry about it now. We can look out for each other." It was too soon to talk her into going away—she'd just think he was blowing her off.

"Exactly."

After a while he said: "I guess the first thing we need is a phone. I don't want to use a pay phone. How about if we stop at a motel and get a room."

She blushed. "George . . . ."

He quickly said, "I just want the phone." Then he thought, what am I saying? "Well, I guess that's not all I want."

She smiled. He noticed there was a car phone, but decided not to use it. She had probably gotten the car from Maxim.

He wanted to ask what state they were in but that would sound strange to her. He was playing along again. But he wasn't going to worry about it. Within a few minutes they reached a small town. A few blocks into it there was a motel, and they stopped and registered. The night clerk asked for a name and George purposefully said, "George . . . uh . . . Preston." He was able to pay with his credit card. He half expected some kind of attack from Maxim, but none came. Maybe the movie considered the ball to be in George's court.

They parked in the far corner of the lot, so if the bad guys somehow tracked them here they wouldn't know which room to look in. Lacey took her overnight bag from the back seat and they went to the room. Inside, she immediately threw her arms around him and kissed him dramatically. He pulled away and said he'd hurry. She sat on the bed. The room was small and plain. There was a nightstand with a phone and a phone book. He sat on the bed himself and looked through the phone book. It told him they were in upstate New York. First he called 911 and reported the fire; he used his real name but just said he had seen the fire from the road. The woman on the other end of the line, who had a sexy voice, asked him for the specific location. He gave the receiver to Lacey and had her tell the woman. Then he looked up the area code for Washington D.C. and called information. Thorpe worked for a small government organization called the Executive Service. George asked for that, but the number he got gave him an escort service. He hung up, called information again, got the number for the FIA, and called that. Another sexy female voice said: "Foreign Intelligence Agency. May I help you?"

"Hi. This is George Preston. I'd like to get ahold of the Executive Service."

"I don't think you have the right number, sir."

"I don't care. I'm secret agent XZ. I work for the Executive Service. I can't reach them, and I have information of vital importance to the safety of the United States and humanity."

"Can you be more specific?"

"How about this—I'll give you all the information, and then you do what you want."

"Well, that's not how we do this, sir. Perhaps you can come here."

"I don't think so. Would you like the information?"

"Could you hold, please?"

"Okay." He put the receiver on his shoulder. Lacey, sitting next to him, pulled him toward her and gave him a long kiss. Then she moved away a little, still looking at him, and whispered, "I could swim naked in your eyes." He just looked at her and smiled. He felt a little dazed. She got up and went to the bathroom with the overnight bag. He heard something on the receiver, lifted it to his ear, and said: "Yes?"

"Mr. Preston?"

"Yes."

"This is Assistant Director of Operations Robert Flagg. Where are you located, sir?" He had a rural accent.

"Upstate New York."

"I see. Can you tell me where exactly?"

George looked at the phone book. "I don't know the town. Somewhere near St. Petersburg." He heard the shower start.

"That's fine. . . . This call is highly irregular, sir. Can you tell me why you didn't call the Executive Service?"

"It's a very long story. I don't have the number."

Surprised: "You don't . . . . How could you not have the number? Have you forgotten it?"

"Sort of. Would you like the information?"

"I would, but, sir, how can I know this is really George Preston?"

"I don't know. My boss is Elizabeth Stone. I've got a buddy in the FIA named Charlie something . . . . Charlie McGwire." He thought. "This is about Dr. Maxim. He's got a henchman called Iron Fist."

"I see. This . . . this is extremely irregular."

"I understand. How about if . . . ."

"Have they done something to affect your memory, sir?"

"Well . . . you could put it that way. How about if I give you the information and you take it from there? It'd be a good idea to get the message to Elizabeth Stone."

"Would you like us to try to connect you to Mrs. Stone?"

"I don't think so. Can I . . . ?"

Interrupting: "Are you in danger?"

"Not at the moment."

"Where are you calling from?"

"I told you, somewhere near St. Petersburg in New York. Starlight Motel."

"And you're on a motel phone?"

"The phone in my room, yeah."

"Well, that's not safe. I have to tell you, sir, you sound like a civilian, and according to our files George Preston is an experienced operative. You see why I have misgivings?"

"Sure. Look, why don't I just give you . . . ?" There was an explosion outside. George threw the receiver on the bed. Frustrated: "I don't believe it."

Lacey opened the bathroom door a little and stuck her head out. She was dripping wet. "What was that?"

"I don't know. Is there a window in there?"

"Yes."

"Then you better come out here."

"I . . . I'll just put on a robe." She closed the door.

He raised his volume a bit: "Do you have a gun?"

She raised her voice so he could hear her through the door: "Of course. In my bag."

George made sure the room was locked, then picked up the receiver. "Mr. Flagg?"

"Was that an explosion?"

"Yeah." Lacey came out, wearing a robe, towel around her head, holding the little gun she'd used on him before. She sat on the bed again; George sat next to her. To Flagg, he said: "Listen, Sparky, no offense, you seem okay, but I'm just going to give you the information. Do what you want."

"Sir, we can't . . . ."

"No time, man. Want the report? I need a yes or a no."

"Yes."

"Dr. Maxim lived around here somewhere. He's moving so people can't reach him when he does this evil scheme he has. He's moving to an island near Hawaii. And I can't be more specific—that's all he told me about the location. Anyway, he's going to infect all the world's computers with this nasty computer virus, then sell the cure or whatever on disks. You can only use each disk one time. Of course he's gonna stick it to everybody regarding the price. He's got it all set up. A little while ago he burned up his mansion here. I was supposed to be burned up with it, so he figured he could tell me his plan. A woman named Lacey Delight rescued me. It's because of her I can tell you this. And she put herself at great risk to do it. She's a hero. If she's broken any laws at any time, what she did should more than make up for it. Have you got all that?"

"Your call's being taped, sir."

"Right. Pardon me. Anyway, run all that by Elizabeth Stone. I guess you can't know Maxim isn't behind this call. He wouldn't do it this way, but I guess I wouldn't either. Anyway, if she just checks what I'm saying you'll all be okay. And tell her I'm retiring. This spy stuff really isn't my thing anymore." After this phone call, he didn't want to spend another second on the spy crap. He wanted to tell the guy to tell Stone not to waste time and resources looking for him, but telling him that wouldn't do any good. Furthermore, since Maxim might come after him, it might not be a waste of time for the Executive Service to do the same. "I guess that's it. Good luck, Flagg. Thanks for your help. I gotta go."

"Thank you, sir."

"You're welcome." He hung up. He felt a little guilty for ditching his assignment and doing nothing more to save this world from getting screwed by Maxim. But he hadn't taken the assignment, and he wasn't willing to treat this like it was real. In fact, they were lucky he had bothered to make the call.

Lacey: "What are we going to do, George?"

"Uh . . . get dressed and we'll check out that explosion."

"Alright." She went back in the bathroom and closed the door.

He walked over to the bathroom door and opened it. Lacey was taking off her robe; she gasped in surprise. George: "Sorry, honey. I don't want them coming through the window. I won't watch."

She got over her surprise, looked at the window, and smiled. "You're sure this isn't just to see me undressed?"

He smiled. "Maybe a little." She had a great body.

Moving much faster than he'd expected, she dried off and then dressed in faded blue jeans and a navy blue T-shirt. She didn't bother with make-up. She combed her hair, quickly, then faced him and said cheerfully: "There. Now I look like you."

"You look beautiful. We still need to get you a sweatshirt though." He changed the subject: "Okay. How many guns do you have?"

She'd set her gun on her bag. She picked it up. "Just this."

"That's okay. Do you mind if I hold it?" She was probably a better shot, but he wanted to be in front.

"Of course not." She gave it to him.

"Okay. Follow me." He took the safety off, went to the door, and carefully opened it, ready to shoot. No one was there. They walked into the parking lot, and saw what had happened. Her RCP was on fire. The hood and the top were gone, blasted off, and there were pieces of flaming and smoking debris scattered around the lot. A few people had gathered around the car. "I'm sorry, Lacey."

She spoke defiantly: "I'm not. It was *his* car—I don't want it. I was supposed to meet him at the airport. I guess since I didn't arrive he decided to do to me what he does to others who trust him."

"Guy's an asshole."

Her accent got thicker: "Exactly." The people who'd gathered around the car were looking at them.

George: "We shouldn't stay here. Let's get your stuff and go. We'll hitchhike out of town."

She leaned against him and said softly, "Okay."

They turned around. They'd left the door open. Now the room looked different. George laughed.

She asked: "What is it?"

They walked back toward the room. George thought quickly. This was his chance. "Listen, I don't think we need to hitchhike anywhere. I'm gonna go somewhere. Do you want to come with me?"

She took his hand. "Yes. But I don't understand."

They were at the door now. He pushed it wide open. Inside was what appeared to be a cartoon room. It looked like the private library of a wealthy man; there were lots of bookshelves, soft chairs, and wood.

Lacey: "What is this?"

"I'm not sure . . . ." He looked at her. "Do you trust me?"

"I trust you."

He could explain later. They were still holding hands. Do it, he thought. "Then hold on tight, and when I say 'now,' we step through. Ready?"

"Yes."

"Now!" Holding her hand, moving with her, he stepped through the doorway.

# CHAPTER 9

George, as he crossed the threshold, felt the hand that was holding Lacey's close on itself. He quickly turned his head; she was gone. He looked back—the doorway he'd stepped through was gone. He looked around. He couldn't believe it. "You motherfuckers!" He kicked over a chair, then ran to a wall of bookshelves and swept books onto the floor. He loved books but he wanted to trash the room. He perceived, not paying attention, that his body was cartoonish like everything else. It was all fairly realistic, though, like an adventure cartoon for kids. He was still holding Lacey's gun. He fired it randomly at books until it was out of bullets, then threw it at other books. He kicked over a coffee table. He kicked a pile of books. He pulled down on some drapes but they stayed put. Frustrated, he grabbed a stool and hurled it at the drapes. It hit the drapes, breaking the window behind them, and fell to the floor. He kicked it across the room, then pulled the drapes aside and looked out—he was several stories up, in a city; it was day.

Tearing up the room was pointless. He wanted Sullok. On the other side of the room was a closed door. He walked quickly across the room and opened it—there was a hallway with a railing, beyond which was an open area. From the open area he heard voices. In control of himself, but determined to give it back to the handlers and to Sullok, he walked into the hallway. He heard, "That's him, Stephen!"

Then Sullok's voice, saying, "I know." A few steps down the hall took George to a wide staircase that curved elegantly downward to a large room. In the room, in various poses, were men and women in superhero costumes. George was in a comic book world. Sullok leaned against a wall next to what looked like a headless blue and white robot. He held what appeared to be the head. George recognized the robot and head as the powered armor for the hero Dreadnought, presumably Sullok's identity now. Sullok looked up at him. "I'm sorry, George."

George nodded, walking down the stairs. "Where's Lacey?"

"I don't know."

George kept coming. He gave Sullok a chance to break character: "Do you know what I'm talking about?"

Sullok shook his head.

"Bullshit. If you don't bring Lacey to me, we've got something to settle."

Sullok set the head on the mantle behind him and moved away from the wall. "Okay." He seemed genuinely sorry.

A man dressed like an old-time stage magician, including top hat and cape, stepped forward and held up his hand, directing his palm at George. Sullok: "No. It's between us." The magician looked at him and, reluctantly, lowered his hand.

A woman in a dark purple bodysuit and black boots, with long, full red hair, said: "Stephen, he doesn't know what he's saying! You've . . . !"

Sullok: "Shut up. It's between us." To George: "If you want to fight, then we fight. Either way, you're okay by me."

George had reached the base of the stairs. This room was a lot like the library, but huge. He stopped. "Thank you. But I owe you one for Lacey."

Sullok nodded. George strode toward him, and made his hands into fists. Sullok moved to an open area. The others gave them room.

George covered the remaining ground between them, and swung at Sullok's jaw. Sullok jerked back, but George still caught his chin. George hit him again, in the stomach; Sullok hit George's face. They continued to trade punches; George went off-balance and fell. Sullok backed up. George quickly got up. "Don't take it easy on me!" He was bleeding. He nodded to himself, then ran at Sullok, and they traded punches again. It wasn't like a comic-book fight—it was a lot of short punches, not a few big ones. George lost his balance and went down again. Again Sullok backed away. George got up, tired, breathing heavily. "If you'd gone down I'd have gotten on top of you. That's how I fight." He paused to get his breath. If Sullok went down now, though, George would let him up. "One more thing. I won't do it now, but the next time I get the chance I'll kill you."

Sullok nodded. "Let's fight, George." George waded in again. He fared even worse than before—Sullok was wearing down a little; George had worn down a lot. He went down again. Sullok: "Maybe you ought to stop."

George: "No." He got up. He remembered that he didn't like those scenes in movies in which the hero took a terrible beating but kept coming because he was such a courageous guy. He went in again, and hit Sullok with a good punch to the jaw. Sullok took one step back; George tried to press his advantage. Sullok quickly regained the upper hand. A few punches later, George was out.

He woke up; he was on the floor, a throw pillow under his head. The red-haired woman in the purple bodysuit was putting bandages on his face. She smiled at him. He closed his eyes. Was this his new love interest? He didn't even want to bother to be polite. The women couldn't seem to resist him in these worlds. He hadn't dated in a while in his real life, to which he wanted very much to return. He went back to sleep. If he was somewhere else when he woke up, that was okay.

He woke up in a large, comfortable bed in a large bedroom. The bed even had a canopy over it. It was still a comic book world. He heard yelling and assorted breaking noises somewhere, not close but not far away either. It was probably a battle. Maybe some bad guy had gotten into the Enforcers' base. That was the name of the "team." He remembered these superheroes from when he'd read comics; he'd stopped reading them about 15 years ago, when he was 12 or 13. Actually, the costumes and the way everything looked seemed like the comic world of that era. He knew comic books had changed dramatically since then. Were they getting all of these worlds out of him somehow, basing them on his memories? Whatever; he didn't want to think about it. And regarding these Enforcers, screw them. They could fight their own battle. He tried to go back to sleep, but couldn't. Then he had to piss. He got out of bed. He was wearing just his white boxer shorts, but the rest of his clothes were folded and sitting on the end of the bed. They'd undressed him and he'd slept through it—that surprised him. He'd been in worse shape than he'd thought. But no matter. He looked around the big room, saw an open door to a bathroom, went in, and pissed. The bathroom, unsurprisingly, was large and elegant, one of the nicest he'd ever been in. In the mirror he saw that his face had several large bandages on it. He yawned, walked out, and got dressed. His dark green sweatshirt had blood on it, which he didn't mind. But what should he do now?

He decided he should just walk out of the Enforcers' base and do his own thing. He didn't want to mess with them anymore. And he wouldn't sneak out—he'd do his best to go to the front door by the most direct route. He wasn't in the mood to take part in or even see the battle, but he wouldn't avoid it. He walked out of the bedroom into a hallway. He could hear the battle below him; he assumed it was in the room where he'd had the fistfight with Sullok. He found a stairway and went down it. It took him to the hallway above the main room, in which the battle was in fact taking place. Walking unhurriedly along the hall, George took it all in. Enforcers were paired off with villains he vaguely recognized. Of course, most of the fighters were excellent physical specimens, and they tended to wear form-fitting costumes. Much of the room was in ruins, with splintered furniture and smashed objects of art everywhere, though on the other hand much was still intact. The battle was quite loud. In addition to crashes, grunts, and the sounds of punches and kicks, the combatants traded vigorous insults. One George picked out was: "You've slowed, Dr. Light! Too bad!" He liked that. He looked among the combatants. He couldn't see Dreadnought. Despite himself, he looked for his redheaded girlfriend, and saw that she was fighting a creature that had metallic skin with tufts of stiff black hair coming out of it here and there. His girlfriend looked great. George knew female superhero costumes had gotten more provocative since the mid '80s, but she looked terrific, all the same. A few of the heroes and villains were flying, including the magician. This man noticed George, and then dramatically threw his cape over the head of his foe—a creature with a sexy female body and the head of a lizard. Then he flew up to George. Hovering in mid-air, he removed a vial from an inside pocket of his jacket and handed it to George. "We need you, Man-o-War! Drink!"

George said, "Thank you." The vial contained a purple liquid that bubbled a little. He took out the black rubber stopper, then paused. "Where's Dreadnought?"

"Your cousin had to go to China to help Captain Steel! There's no time! Drink!"

His cousin. Whatever. "Thanks. Don't mind if I do." He drank it all down—it tasted like carbonated medicine. He tossed the vial and the rubber stopper over the railing. He felt energy coursing through him. He felt the wounds on his face heal. He laughed and shook his head. He started to float. There was a kind of purple glow around him. He tore the bandages off his face. He turned to the magician, smiling. "Thank you!"

"You're welcome! Now let's kick some tail!" Now George remembered the guy's name—Magicko. Magicko flew back into the battle and confronted a blond woman—not flying—wearing an opaque green fishnet bodysuit. George flew up and down the hall, then made a circle in mid-air. Some kind of energy blast hit him from behind. He turned and saw a fat man on the floor of the main room, wearing some sort of metal exoskeleton. The exoskeleton featured a glowing red disk, about the size of a dinner plate, over the guy's chest. Under the exoskeleton he wore pants and boots but no shirt; his belly was hairy. He was laughing. In a gravelly voice, he said, "Don't you want to play, Man-o-War?"

George felt power surging all over his body, but especially in his hands. Still floating, he made fists, pointed them at the red disk, and concentrated on directing energy at it. A wide purple ray, or something, surged out from his fists and into the disk. He poured on the ray; the bad guy said "No!" fearfully, and there was an explosion. The blast sent the guy back through a wall. George flew over the railing and down so he could see through the wall opening. He heard a masculine voice: "Way to go, buddy!" Through the wall opening, he saw the bad guy, his exoskeleton badly damaged, struggling to get up.

Someone threw someone else toward George; George flew upward to avoid the guy being thrown, who slammed into a couch, knocking it over, and came to rest sprawled on the floor. George had had enough of the battle. He flew through a doorway to yet another hallway. As he did, a female voice yelled, "George!?" The voice conveyed painful confusion and disappointment, as if the speaker was witnessing a heartbreaking act of betrayal and couldn't believe her eyes. George actually did feel guilt pangs, but he didn't stop. He thought about Lacey and most of the guilt went away. Maybe it was the red-haired woman. He could stay and help, get attached to her, then go or be taken to the next world and wonder what her fate was. Did all of these worlds exist before and after he was in them? He didn't want to think about it. He decided not to bother looking for the front door. He flew through the closest doorway, which took him into a big bedroom; he flew across the bedroom and then with a crash through a large window.

Floating outside the window, he watched the pieces of glass fall several stories to the street below. He yelled a warning to the people on the sidewalk, though they would probably have gotten out of the way anyway. Some of them pointed at him, not many. Superheroes were commonplace here. He waved at them, then flew along the street from his current height. He was about five stories up. He'd been in St. Louis hundreds of times, but he hadn't been this high up in a city very often. He'd been in airplanes a couple of times, and he'd liked it, but the view he had now was unique. The fact that it was all cartoonish made it even better. He loved the color. There was, unfortunately, a sameness to the buildings. They varied, but much less than buildings in real cities. And this city lacked the details of real ones. But you couldn't have everything. He followed the busy street, watching the cars and the people. He looked up at blue sky and clouds. It felt like spring.

He flew a few stories higher. If the potion wore off suddenly, he'd fall to the street and appear in the next world, or maybe his apartment. He couldn't be sure, but he was willing to take the chance. It felt good to put distance between himself and the Enforcers. It would have been very nice to have sex with the redhead (especially since she was cartoonish), but it wouldn't have been worth it. Sex would have been only a possibility anyway, if he remembered his comics right. It was okay.

He couldn't remember a superhero like this, which didn't mean there hadn't been one. He liked the powers. He could easily fly as fast as the cars were moving. He speeded up—that was easy too. He wondered what his limit was. He flew higher, until he was above the tallest building. There was an airplane far away from him; otherwise he had the sky to himself. He remembered the Enforcers were based in Chicago. He flew in a random direction, at a moderate pace. He accelerated, gradually, and kept at it until he was going extremely fast. He noticed Lucas Field. He accelerated even more. The buildings changed, becoming shorter and less attractive. Maybe he was leaving the city proper. He pushed it to his limit, scaring himself despite the lack of anything to collide with, despite the fact that death probably wouldn't be permanent. He had no idea how fast he was going; he just knew it was a little scary. The area below him still looked more or less urban, but he knew he was past the city limits. He stopped suddenly and started to fly back at a relaxed pace. He hadn't seen Lake Michigan yet—he'd check that out.

He remembered he was low on money. Still flying, he took his wallet out and counted his funds—$28.35. And he had no idea how many worlds he had ahead of him. This would be a perfect time to get money; he wouldn't have superpowers again. Of course, he hadn't thought about it before, but he could hold up a liquor store in any world anytime he could get a gun, which seemed to be often. It'd be more interesting to do it now, though. He flew lower and looked for a likely target. He felt guilt pangs again. He could imagine himself as a citizen, getting robbed by a popular superhero. He fought down the guilt. He thought about Dr. Maxim and almost being burned alive, and the guilt went away.

He wouldn't fool around with a bank. He didn't really need much, and couldn't conveniently carry much. He wasn't sure what his best target would be. After a couple of blocks he spotted a liquor store and flew in through the open door. It wasn't pretty—there were bars on the windows, a little trash on the floor. The guy behind the counter looked like a jerk, and about half of the customers looked like alcoholics, at least to George. He let his feet touch the ground, then willed away the floating, so he had to support himself with his legs. That felt strange now.

The guy behind the counter gave him a big smile. "Hey, it's Man-o-War! How's it going?"

George: "Okay." He would have preferred that the guy be rude.

Another guy grabbed George's shoulder, meaning to be friendly. "Hey, George, how they hangin'?"

George could smell whiskey on the guy's breath. Nervous, he said, "Hangin' good." He couldn't do it, not to these people. He gently pulled his shoulder free. "Look, I gotta go. Have a good one." He floated off the floor, then flew out, having to maneuver awkwardly around a heavy middle-aged woman in the doorway.

"Watch it!" she said, rudely.

George, responding in kind: "Yeah, yeah."

As he flew upward, he heard someone inside the place yell, "See ya, Georgie!"

He found a Burger Boss a few blocks away and flew into that. There weren't many customers. A teenaged boy at the counter said, "Hey, Man-o-War!"

"Hey." There was no one in line. George put his feet on the floor and again willed away the floating. He approached the boy. "Look, I don't mean to be rude. I don't know quite how to do this. But I need some money from your drawer."

The boy looked puzzled, then laughed. "What are you talkin' about?"

"I need some money." He paused, then added, "I'm kind of in a hurry."

The boy was still puzzled, but he wasn't laughing now. "I don't get it, George. I can't give you the money."

"I'd rather not destroy the cash register. Please give me the money now and I won't."

A guy in his mid twenties, a little younger than George, came up behind the boy. The guy said: "I got it, Ed." The boy stood aside. To George, the guy said: "The money's not yours. What do you need it for?"

"I can't explain. I don't need much. Say the twenties from the drawer. I kind of need them now or I'll destroy the register."

The man looked at him, frowning. Then he pushed a button on the register and the drawer opened. "You need 'em that bad, you got 'em! But I'm calling the cops!" People in this world tended to speak in exclamations, but the guy still managed to seem disappointed. This irritated George. He didn't hold anything against the guy, but he resented the handlers even more. The guy took out a short stack of twenties and handed them over.

"Thank you." Everyone in the place was quiet while he walked out. Just outside the doorway, he turned and asked, "What year is it?"

No one answered for a few seconds, then the guy who'd handed him the money said, "1983!"

"I thought so." He looked up, then flew. He didn't count the bills. When the money ran out, if it did, he would get more. There were too many bills to fit comfortably in his wallet; he put some there, then folded the rest and put them in the left front pocket of his jeans. He kept going up until he was again above the tallest buildings. He still wanted to see Lake Michigan. If he flew high enough, he would be able to see it regardless of how many miles away it was. Now that he thought about it, he'd like that view, anyway.

He heard a thump. He stopped in mid-air, sighed, and looked around. About 30 yards away, pointed downward at maybe a 50-degree angle to the ground, was a wooden door in a frame. It was just like the door he'd opened to get to the spy world. He wondered what the angle was for. Was there a point to it? It all seemed so arbitrary. He flew under the door, then around it, then he stopped in front of it. Hovering in mid-air, he opened it.

He was looking down at train tracks, in a black and white world. The door was perpendicular to the ground, but about 20 feet up. The tracks ran through level plains; the plains stretched as far as he could see in every direction he could see. The landscape, such as it was, was dull but looked real—unlike the landscape in the Bagby world, different parts of it looked similar but not identical. The ground, for instance, was not completely level. Why 20 feet up? Why not ground level, beside the tracks? He let it go. He stuck one of his hands through the doorway. As it passed across the threshold, it lost its cartoon-ness and became the same black and white—grayness, really, was the impression one got—as the rest of the new world. Instead of a glowing purple aura his hand now had a glowing light gray aura. It was neat. He stuck part of his arm in, then moved his hand and arm back and forth across the threshold. He stuck one of his feet and part of the leg in, and saw the same effect. A train, making no sound, passed under him. Standing on top of the engine, facing back in George's direction, was a slightly built man with short curly hair and freckles. George recognized him. It was the silent film star Plucky O'Neill. This was probably *The Railroad*, his best-known movie. Plucky (who was wearing high-wasted pants and suspenders) saw George and got a surprised look, understated by silent film standards. He leaned forward a little, then back. The train was moving at a fairly good rate, maybe 20 miles per hour. Plucky looked to the left, hesitated, then looked to the right, then back at George. George laughed. He looked down and saw the train speeding along under him. He could easily fly through the doorway, but why should he? He'd gone through every doorway they'd offered him so far. This was a good time to change that. He had nothing against Plucky O'Neill, but he didn't particularly like silent movies. It would be interesting to have superpowers in a different world, but that wasn't reason enough to go through. He looked up—Plucky was still watching him, standing still. The caboose rolled by under George; the train was heading for the horizon. George waved and started to turn; to his surprise, Plucky waved back. Leaving the door open, he flew backward a bit, then turned and flew up and away from the door. After a few seconds he looked over his shoulder—the door was gone.

He looked around. A few people were gathered on the street below him, looking up. One was pointing. Presumably they'd seen the door, but they could just be reacting to him. Screw it. He still wanted to see the lake. He flew up. If Plucky had spoken to him, would he have seen the words appear? He belatedly looked around to make sure the way was clear of planes. It was. Then he looked down as he flew up, checking out the view. He liked it—everything getting steadily smaller (the people were soon invisible), the larger pattern of the streets becoming more apparent. After a while he could see the lake. He flew upward faster. The view was beautiful and amazing. It all looked and seemed unreal yet real. He noticed something out of the corner of his eye, and looked that way. It looked like a giant robot walking between the buildings. It swung its arm into a building, and George could hear the impact. He hesitated, looked around—pointlessly—, then flew toward it for a better look. He kept his eyes on it. It kept walking, and occasionally, arbitrarily, did massive damage to a building. It moved with less agility, and more slowly, proportionally, than a human, but not by much. As he got closer he could see it had a face, and wore a contemptuous expression. To his surprise, as he got still closer he saw that its expression was not fixed. The expression didn't change quickly or smoothly—it was like early '80s computer animation for facial expressions. Nor did the type of expression change. It just made small adjustments in its sneer.

George felt a fairly powerful dislike of the thing, whatever it was. It reinforced this feeling by stopping its progress to stoop and pick up a small truck, then crushing the truck and tossing it over its shoulder. Its face changed to register delight. George wasn't far now. In fact, the robot, or whatever, looked at him, still smiling. George hadn't wanted to bother with fighting it, but now he thought, I'll bite. He flew directly at it, very fast. He held his fists in front of himself and concentrated, sending a wide purple ray at the robot. The ray hit its cheek. George adjusted his aim so the ray hit its eye. The smile went away, replaced by a look of anger and pain. It raised a hand. George, excited, speeded up. The center of the robot's palm glowed orange. George, who felt terrific, stopped firing the ray, speeded up still more, and changed his angle of flight. Some kind of orange ray erupted out of the robot's palm, but it missed him. He flew downward but kept flying toward it, laughing. He blasted it with the purple ray again, hitting its chest. It held out its other palm, the center of which glowed. George changed his angle of flight again, a little sideways and further downward— he and the robot were between buildings, which limited his options somewhat. It fired the orange ray again. He caught some of the ray this time, briefly. It caused him some pain but didn't knock him out. The purple glow apparently protected him. The pain didn't last. This was fun. He flew on a path to go between its widespread legs; as he did he blasted its metallic belly. He was briefly tempted to blast it between the legs (there was nothing there, of course), but didn't—that would be juvenile. It moved a hand so the palm was toward him; again the center glowed. He did a J-turn but got nailed by the orange ray anyway. He flew between two buildings to take himself out of the line of fire. He heard a crunching, crashing noise. It was taking out part of a building to get a shot at him. He flew straight up, planning to nail it as soon as he cleared the top of that building. Then the upper third of the building broke away and started to fall toward him; he flew down and to the side, managing to avoid it. But then the robot hit him from behind with some kind of blue lightning. This threw him against another building, dazing him; he fell. He recovered his senses, and could hear the robot laughing. He started flying again. He saw that the robot had thrown its head back to laugh.

He heard something new, sounding a little like a jet. He flew at the robot again, firing his ray at its head. Above the robot he saw something vaguely like a flying saucer, but ovoid rather than circular, with jet propulsion. Probably the Enforcers. It hovered above the robot, then hit the robot with a yellow ray that had, ridiculously, white spheres in it. George fired his purple ray again, though now he could feel himself weakening. The robot ignored him; it looked overhead, raising both its hands, and fired the orange ray from each palm. Both rays hit the flying ship. Still firing, the robot roared triumphantly. The ship, still getting hit, flew between buildings, seeking to escape the rays. George flew upward, steadily firing his own ray—he wanted a better angle. The robot pointed a fist at him and fired blue lightning, but it was paying most of its attention to the ship, and it missed him. Then the ship was out of the line of fire.

The robot turned all its attention to George, still using the lightning. He flew up over a building and down the other side, the lightning narrowly missing him. He flew down almost to the ground and then around the building. There were a few people on the ground. One of them yelled, "Pour it on, Man-o-War!" George waved, quickly. When he got the robot back in view, he got a surprise. It was surrounded by flying Enforcers, and the ship was back in action. George immediately joined in, firing his ray, which was, however, even weaker, and weakening steadily. Nevertheless, though George was losing power, the Enforcers clearly had the upper hand. The robot fought back, swatting at heroes and shooting rays at them, but it was obviously in deep trouble. It didn't even bother with George; still firing, he flew up toward its head. Then the robot lowered its hands, just letting the various colorful rays hit it. It roared, and then said grandly: "Impressive display, small ones! But let's see how you fare in my dimension!" Then it made a great V of its arms. There was a tremendous explosion—George felt nothing, but saw green light all around him.

Then the light blinked away, and George was in another world— though not in the sense he'd been thinking of since he'd started these adventures—this was still a comic book. The robot was here, smiling broadly. The Enforcers and their ship were also here. The sky was red, and there were four purple suns. The planet surface was blue dirt. There were buildings, the tallest only a few stories tall, which looked to George like little castles made out of stucco. The atmosphere felt thick; George could breath, but not easily. The strangest thing to him was the look of the inhabitants of this place. They looked like reptilian humanoids, with flippers instead of feet. They were light green, wore no clothing, and seemed to swim through the thick air. They looked with curiosity at the Enforcers, but not at the robot. George was still glowing, faintly, but now he glowed pink. He shrugged, raised an eyebrow, pointed his fists at the robot, and concentrated. There was no ray. He tried to say, 'Cocksucker,' but couldn't. He gagged on the air and coughed violently. The other Enforcers were having similar problems.

"Now," said the robot, beaming, "this should be interesting!" The reptile people watched but swam away as they did. George gave the robot the finger. He tried to fly and succeeded, but he was very slow. The robot continued, looking around, "Who should I start with?" The Enforcers were obviously confused. George tried the ray again; it was useless. The robot looked at him. "Ah! The brave little purple man!" It stepped toward him. The other Enforcers and the ship flew, slowly, in the direction of the robot's head; those Enforcers who couldn't fly could swim through the air more or less like the reptile people. George also flew toward its head. He wanted to yell, but gave it the finger again instead. The robot took another step and reached for him. He tried to evade its hand but was much too slow. It caught him and brought him close to its face. It said, still smiling, "Goodbye, purple man!"

George mouthed, "Fuck me." It crushed him.

# CHAPTER 10

George started to yell, then cut himself off. The pain of being crushed had been severe but very brief. Once he was in this new world, the pain was gone completely. He had yelled only from the memory of it. He was in a black and white world, in a bedroom. The black and white was different from that of the Plucky O'Neill world, sharper. He was black and white too, of course. He was glowing white, faintly, but that faded to nothing in a couple of seconds—he didn't react quickly enough to test what was left of his powers in the new world. The room was clean for the most part. The bed was made. There was a wooden desk and chair, a dresser, a nightstand, a small bookshelf with assorted hardbound books, a second wooden chair, and a clothes hamper. There was a window with curtains and blinds, and two doors. A couple of pictures hung on the walls. One was of George as a teenager, in a football uniform, holding a football, smiling. The other showed George in his early twenties in a family portrait, with a little brother, maybe 11 or 12, who looked slightly rebellious, but cute, and parents, mid to late forties, conservative but likable. The father and sons wore suits and ties, the mom wore a dress, and all had big smiles. The desk had a record player and a radio on it. On top of the bookshelf was a small, intricate model airplane. Hanging on the desk chair was a college-looking jacket with white leather arms. He picked it up—it had four S's sewn to the front. He dropped it. On the bed was what looked to him like a kind of overnight bag. It was open—inside it were textbooks, notebooks, folders, and other school supplies. It was all terribly '50s-ish, much more so than the *Allen* world. He was apparently a college student, maybe home for the weekend. He was too old in real life to be a traditional college student. And that was the kind of college student he'd be here, not a 27-year-old graduate student.

There was a knock at the door. A mom-like voice said, "Honey, are you okay?"

He said, "Fine, Mom."

"You sure? I heard you yell."

"I'm sure. I stubbed my toe."

"Well, alright. Come downstairs when you get settled in." He heard her walk away.

He sat on the bed. He didn't like '50s sitcoms, which this apparently was. He didn't hate them either; they just weren't his cup of tea. As a kid he'd liked them a little. Actually, with all the craziness of these worlds, and his just having died an unpleasant death, it was sort of comforting to be here. Much more so than the *Allen* world. The movie *Allen* had been intended to be a little creepy. That wasn't true of these sitcoms. On the other hand, if he could have chosen another world, he wouldn't have chosen this. What was their game? The last world was one he had in fact chosen, though since the time he'd asked for it and the time he'd gotten it the handlers had totally alienated him. The world before that, the spy world, wasn't one he would have asked for, and he hadn't particularly liked being in it. Except for Lacey, of course, and he'd lost her. Before that was the *Allen* world, which had interested him. He wouldn't have thought to ask for it, but he had kind of liked the sport of escaping. Before that was a world he'd detested, that of Panama Johnson. He'd liked the novel, but not the world, and he would not have asked for it. Before that the Bagby minimalist world, which he had disliked even more. Before that a world he'd ordered like a pizza and loved, the Pistol Kramer world. Before that— what was before that? A commercial—he had liked that a little. Before that the cult TV show, *Hidden Agendas*. He had mixed feelings about the show—he certainly wasn't part of the cult. What he'd liked best about that world was shooting Sullok. Before that had been the rainy city. What the hell was that supposed to be? Science fiction, but not just any science fiction. Sort of a combination of sci-fi and film noir. Now that he thought about it, he'd seen a few movies like that and liked them. He hadn't asked for it, but he'd chosen to step into it. There hadn't been much about it to like. He hadn't been there long, but it'd been the least pleasant world, mostly because he'd believed it was real and that death there would be permanent. Of course, he still didn't know just how real or unreal these worlds were.

It occurred to him that the handlers seemed to be running out of ideas. They'd been sending him to pretty hackneyed worlds since *Allen*. Spy movies, superhero comic books, '50s sitcoms—all had been satirized to death. Of course, these weren't satires. If something outside the conventions happened in any of these worlds, it was because of him. He was the only wildcard in any of these decks, other than Sullok. And Sullok always seemed to stay in character, though he might talk in code. Even in the last world, Sullok's behavior could have been explained by some kind of plot line George didn't know about. What was their point? Why a '50s sitcom? Why not all worlds he loved? Why not all worlds he hated? Or all worlds he had a lot of interest in, or all worlds he had no interest in? Why do this at all? Why do it to him and not someone else?

He wasn't particularly helping himself now by analyzing it. He didn't have any answers. He let it go. He got up and checked the other door. It was a closet, with lots of dress shirts and pants hanging up, and assorted junk on the floor and on the overhead shelf. He went to the window and pulled the blinds. It was daytime; it hadn't occurred to him to wonder whether it was day or night. He saw a nice backyard, mowed, with a couple of trees, a flowerbed, and a garden. A baseball glove lay by one of the trees. There was a white picket fence. Other, similar yards were visible. It was a nice scene, topped off, as usual, by blue—technically, light gray—sky, and just a few clouds, though it all looked a little strange and not quite as nice in black and white. He heard a song start in the next room, just beyond his closet. It was a rock and roll song he faintly recognized, not one of the '50s songs that you still heard in 2000. It wasn't bad though. It was about a teenaged boy trying to get a girl's attention. Presumably the little brother from the picture was in the next room playing a record.

George's sweatshirt had dried blood on it. He hadn't cared about that in the last world, but he couldn't wear it like that here without people bothering him about it. He took it off and threw it on the bed, then looked in the closet for a shirt. In black and white, there wasn't much to distinguish them but the patterns. He found one he liked, with thick vertical stripes, white alternating with a dark color. He put it on; it fit perfectly. But it looked very wrong with jeans and sneakers. He'd figured he didn't care about that when he'd picked it out, but he did. He looked in the dresser and found a long-sleeved shirt in a light color, with no buttons and no collar. Close enough. He took off the nice shirt, dropped it on the floor, and put on the other one.

He also needed another shower, and another shave. He stepped out into the hall. It was bland, with a few family pictures and a painting of flowers hanging on the walls. He went in the opposite direction from the music; he heard a door open behind him. "George!"

He turned. There was the kid from the picture, now in his mid teens. He was beaming, very happy to see his big brother. He even looked a little like George, though he was better looking. The girls watching the show would love him. George said, "Hi."

The song was ending—surprisingly, the singer had failed to get the girl's attention, and decided to move on. The resolution worked for George. The kid's face changed a little, becoming mock-serious, and he sang along on the last line: " '. . . I'd rather drive a truck.' "

George smiled. "How ya been?"

"I've been alright. I would have knocked on your door, but I didn't want to disturb you. You know, with you being a grown-up college guy and all."

He was a nice kid. "Thanks. I appreciate that. So . . . what have you been doing?"

"Oh, you know. I do stuff with the guys. I do homework. . . . I'm getting pretty good on the guitar."

George didn't think he'd seen this show, but a few bells were going off—he'd heard of it. So it was an actual show, which meant the kid looking like him was just a coincidence, unless that was one of the reasons they'd sent him here. He said: "I'll bet you are. The girls like that?"

The kid looked down, a little embarrassed. "I don't know. Maybe. I don't do it for the girls. I do it for the music."

"Nothing wrong with that. Anyway, I better take a shower."

Kid, surprised: "Now?"

"Yeah. I need one."

"Well, okay. I'll see you later."

"See ya later." He went into the bathroom and closed the door. It reminded him of his grandmother's bathroom. Like hers, it was completely clean. There was a bathtub on ornamental legs, with a showerhead above it, and a curtain you could pull around the tub. He undressed, then realized he needed a clean washcloth and towel. He wrapped a used towel around himself and went into the hall, which, fortunately, was empty. He opened the nearest door. It was a closet with, among other things, towels and washcloths in it. He grabbed one of each and returned to the bathroom. Now he knew who the kid was—Mickey Reynolds. Reynolds had in fact had a brief career as a rock and roll star; his big hit was "Bonny Blue." He hadn't had a very good life after that, though he was still alive in 2000. George started the water, dropped the used towel on the floor, hung the clean towel on a rack, hung the washcloth on the rod holding the shower curtain, tested to make sure the water wasn't too hot or cold, and got in the shower. He was sorry about Mickey. The kid seemed awfully nice. Of course, he had really been talking to the character, also named Mickey but with a different last name. (And in this world, since George was his brother, Mickey's last name had to be Preston.) Whatever. George was sorry anyway.

He hurried through the shower, figuring the hot water wouldn't last. The shampoo looked funny and there was no conditioner. He of course closed his eyes to wash his hair; opening them again to a black and white world was strange. And it was strange seeing everything in black and white as he felt the water hit him and went through the routine of taking a shower. He finished, got out, and started drying off. There was a knock at the door. George: "Yes?"

Mom: "Are you taking a shower?"

"Just finishing."

"At six o'clock?"

"I needed one."

"Well hurry, dear. Your dinner's getting cold."

George didn't want to eat here. "I'll be down pretty soon."

"Alright."

He finished drying and got dressed. Then he found a razor, not disposable, in the medicine cabinet above the sink. There was also a cake of some kind of soap and a brush in a porcelain container, all of which he could use to make shaving cream, but he wanted no part of that. He used the hand soap to make lather, put that on his face, and shaved. It worked well enough. When he was finished he went back to his own room and found a comb in a dresser drawer. There was no mirror in his room so he went back to the bathroom and combed his hair. Then he realized he had to use the toilet. He went back to his bedroom and looked for something to read. The bookshelf had some classics on it; he picked *Captured*, by John Thomas Richardson, a well-written adventure novel he'd read a long time ago. He hoped he wouldn't be a character in it later. A male voice, presumably his father's, called up from downstairs: "George?" The voice was slightly confused, unlike most of the dads in the '50s sitcoms George had seen.

He opened his bedroom door and called down: "I've got to use the bathroom." There was no answer. He went into the bathroom and did his business while he browsed through the book. When he was done he washed his hands, went back to his room, tossed *Captured* on the bed, and went downstairs. The stairs took him into a living room. The dad was in an armchair with a newspaper; Mickey was standing. The mom came in from the kitchen, a dish towel in her hands. The room was very clean, and in general just like he expected. The three of them looked at him. The dad wore a suit, the mom a nice dress and pearls. Mickey was dressed casually. The dad set down his paper and said, "Well, there he is."

George: "Hi."

Dad: "Boy starts going to college, you never see him."

George sat on the couch. "Well, you're seeing me."

Mickey: "He's not a boy, Dad. Neither am I."

The dad laughed. "I stand corrected."

Mom: "Your dinner's getting cold, sweetheart. Come on in and eat."

George didn't want to eat here. More importantly, he realized he was setting himself up to lose his sweatshirt. If something happened to send him to the next world and he didn't have it on him, it was gone. "Be right back." He ran up the stairs.

Dad, puzzled: "Well where are you going, Son?"

"Be right back." He grabbed the sweatshirt off the bed and walked back downstairs with it balled up in his hands.

Dad: "What was that all about?"

George: "Uh . . . I had to get my sweatshirt. I gotta go."

Dad: "What?"

Mom: "Aren't you going to eat your dinner, dear?" She sounded a little hurt.

Once again, George felt guilty, then got mad at the handlers for laying the guilt on him. It may not have been their intent, but he didn't mind blaming them anyway. "I can't eat . . . ." Suddenly he didn't want to call her "Mom." She wasn't his mom. This wasn't his family.

Mickey: "Where you going?"

George: "Uh . . . I gotta meet somebody." Once the words were out of his mouth, he realized he'd lied. Then he thought, why shouldn't I lie? What could be more of a lie than pretending to be part of their family?

Mickey, big smile: "You're going to meet *Sarah*."

"Maybe. Gotta go." He strode to the door, opened it, stepped through, and closed it behind him. He'd thought they'd say something, but they didn't. Fuck it. Had he hurt their feelings? Well, it was a big fucking joke anyway.

He walked down a narrow sidewalk to the street, then down the street. There was a broad sidewalk, but he walked in the street itself. It was beautiful out, in the seventies. He didn't need the sweatshirt. He tied it around his waist, which he had a habit of doing in real life. A big '50s car drove by; the driver was a forty-something guy in a suit. The driver honked and waved; George waved back. He was feeling very relieved. He'd probably never see any of them again. He certainly wouldn't if he had anything to say about it. He felt offended on behalf of his own family, who weren't cute or perfect. His real father, named Robert, called Bob, was totally unlike the guy in the house, and also very different from George. Just under six feet tall and heavy, he was sociable and loud. While George didn't date much, his dad had gone through lots of girlfriends in his bachelor days, and liked to point this out occasionally. George's mom, Claire, was a small woman, intellectual, quiet, but with a bad temper. Once, in front of George and his sister, she'd slapped his father so hard the man's nose had bled. George's older sister, Ginny, had been bossy when they were growing up. That wasn't such a big deal though; they'd gotten along well, anyway.

He reached the end of his street; there was a T intersection. He turned left—east—to get the sun behind him. He reflected that this was what he always did. He went to a world, starting out in the thick of it. Then he extricated himself from whatever was going on and just walked away. Well, not always, but a lot. On the other hand, what was wrong with that? It seemed like a pretty good idea.

The houses didn't look identical, but they looked similar. If someone was making the point that life in the suburbs in the '50s was too conformist, he got it. Actually, though, whatever the handlers' point was, the people who made this show hadn't wanted to make any such point. Furthermore, or nevertheless, he supposed that being in entertainment, the people who made the show were relatively liberal for their time. Or maybe not—anyway, screw it.

He followed the road. He had plenty of daylight left. Anyway, what did it matter if it got dark on him? He could rent a room or sleep outdoors. His family here might worry, but he didn't consider them real. They certainly weren't his family. He saw a few cars drive by. Some of the drivers honked and waved; he always waved back. He saw a guy in a suit walking his dog. The guy said, cheerfully, "Hello, George," and the dog barked a greeting. George said, "Hello."

The street intersected another that a sign told him was Main Street. He turned onto it, a little curious but also thinking it might be a pain. There was plenty of traffic, by both cars and pedestrians. He loved the cars—some huge, all big, plenty of convertibles, lots of chrome, tailfins, and hood ornaments. It was like being at a classic auto show. A lot of people greeted him; apparently he was pretty popular. A big dumb guy on foot, in a jacket like the one in George's room, with letters sewn on it and leather arms, wanted to shoot the shit with him. George nicely got away, saying he had to meet someone.

Guy: "Oh . . . . *Sarah* . . . ."

"Well, you know . . . ."

"Oh yeah, *I* know. See ya, George."

"Not if I see you first." They both laughed. The big guy seemed alright, anyway.

George got enough funny looks to figure out that he wasn't supposed to wear a sweatshirt tied around his waist. He thought of leaving it there to sort of thumb his nose at the world, then decided he didn't want to do that. He took it off. With all the blood on it he still couldn't wear it normally. He didn't want to carry it, but would if he had to. He decided to wear it like a cape, putting the sleeves over his shoulders and tying them, with the blood-stained part against his back. He'd worn sweaters and jackets that way before, and it seemed sort of '50s-ish to him. There were no more funny looks.

Another passing car honked. He turned and waved. It was Sullok, in an unusually big, very cool car. His hair was hidden under a hat, and he wore a suit. He had slowed down. He gave George a big, possibly sincere smile and a friendly wave. George turned away and kept walking. He expected Sullok to say something, and he did, in a friendly tone: "Hiya, George." George ignored him. Sullok speeded up again. He'd been pretty good about it, sort of checking in without thrusting himself on George. Sullok had also handled himself like a gentleman in the last world. But that didn't make up for everything. And if George was willing to hold Sullok accountable for things that happened generally in these worlds—and he was—then Sullok had plenty to answer for in these last two worlds, as well. And he apparently wasn't going to answer for anything, at any time.

Most of the businesses were closed. One that wasn't was a diner, or whatever they called it—a place where teens hung out, where you could get, among other things, ice cream and burgers. The place looked so hackneyed George was somewhat surprised by it—he'd expect something like it in a modern movie imitating '50s sitcoms, but not in a real '50s sitcom. He was thirsty, and curious about the place. He went in. The place had tile, bar stools, chrome all over, a jukebox playing, girls in poodle skirts, and guys in button shirts, most without ties. The guy behind the counter wore a white uniform, a black bow tie, and a white paper hat. George heard a couple hi's and waved; these were mostly teenagers, too young to know his character well. The counter guy—George was suddenly, for some reason, grateful that they had put Sullok on the street instead of behind the counter—said, "What can I do you for, George?"

For no reason he could think of, George suddenly felt creeped out by the whole situation. But he fought it down—he'd just get what he wanted and leave quickly. "Uh . . . how about a Xerxi and a cheeseburger?"

Counter guy, cheerfully: "You got it."

"To go."

The guy hesitated: "To go where?"

"Never mind. My mistake."

The guy put a hamburger patty on the grill, then took a glass much like Sullok had used in the Xerxi world, scooped ice into it, and filled it with cola from a fountain. This really was cola, of course. The guy set it on the counter. Then he went to the grill and deftly made the cheeseburger. He put it on a plate in front of George and said, "Forty cents."

George took out his wallet. He took out a one, then put it back, took out a twenty, and slapped it on the counter. "Keep the change."

The guy was shocked. "George . . . I . . . what are you doing?"

George put a cheerful tone in his voice. "I'm loaded. It's my pleasure. And don't try to give it back to me—I won't take it." He nodded briskly. He was feeling better again.

"Well, thank you. Thank you very much."

"My pleasure. Oh, can I keep the glass for that?"

The guy laughed. "You bet you can." He'd regained his composure; he was very happy. "You rob a bank?"

George laughed and walked out, burger in one hand, glass in the other. Continuing down the road, he more or less wolfed down the okay-tasting cheeseburger. He didn't know what to do with the glass when he was done—he didn't want to leave broken glass on the sidewalk. Actually, now that he thought about it, he did want to do that. This wasn't the real world.

The road went on. He reached the last of the businesses and kept walking. Past the businesses there were no other people on foot and little traffic. The sidewalk ended and he walked on the side of the road. Beyond the businesses were a few houses, spread out, old-looking. Then they ended. He finished his drink, took a piece of ice into his mouth, and hurled the glass violently onto the road. It made a good crash. Ice and glass went all over. He crunched up and swallowed the ice in his mouth, still walking. He could feel the caffeine. The creepiness he'd felt before was totally gone. He felt good.

About five minutes later the road intersected with a two-lane highway, with plenty of traffic. He had definitely walked out of town, and he liked that. He again turned east, and walked along the highway. There was a wide gravel shoulder for him to walk on. Occasionally a car honked, and he waved, automatically, not really paying attention. Then a big light-colored convertible pulled over in front of him. The driver was a young woman with her hair in a ponytail, obviously Sarah. She turned around in the seat, big smile, and waved enthusiastically. "Hi, George!" Her voice was a little squeaky.

He smiled back and walked toward the driver's side of the car. If nothing else, they seemed concerned about his love life. "Hi. How's it going?"

"Great. Want to go for a ride?"

He thought it over quickly. "Sure." He redirected himself toward the passenger's side.

"So what are you doing out here?"

"Just out for a walk. Thought I'd clear my head." He couldn't get the door open.

Her face suddenly became serious. "The doors don't open. *You know*."

He climbed over the door and into the seat. Was she mad about him forgetting? No one was perfect.

"You wanted to clear your head? Is . . . is that because of Sarah?"

That threw him. She checked for oncoming traffic, then pulled back onto the highway. George: "What do you mean?"

"Uh . . . I don't know. Maybe I shouldn't say anything." She was very pretty, with blond hair and full lips, in her early twenties, and she wore a dark, long skirt with a light blouse.

"I . . . what's going on?" He felt a twinge of irritation at his own witlessness.

She kept her eyes on the road. She took a breath. It seemed rude to stare at her; he turned and watched the road too. Finally she said, "You and I have always been friends, right?"

"Sure."

She took another deep breath. "Well, I'm a girl who stands up for her friends. If Sarah Woods thinks she's going to make a fool out of you, she's got another thing coming. That's all I have to say."

George didn't say anything. Then when he saw she was waiting, he said, "Go on." He felt a little hurt, even though this wasn't real—it was like he couldn't help being in character.

"George . . . ." He felt her hand on his arm, then she took his hand and squeezed it. He squeezed in response. "George . . . maybe we should go somewhere and talk." She put her hand back on the wheel. "Is the lake alright?"

"Sure."

Her tone became cheerful and determined. "Great. And remember, no matter what, you can always count on Terry Cannutto."

An Italian name, but no accent, and blond hair. And it was like the handlers were helping him out by telling him her name. "Thanks, Terry. You're a pal."

She smiled. "Don't mention it."

They didn't say anything for a while. Soon she turned off the highway, then along another road, then onto a gravel road that took them to a lake. She pulled up to a grassy area where about ten other cars were parked. A few of the occupants of the other cars were talking. Most were making out. Terry, turning her car off: "I just hope we don't see them here."

George, as they turned to face each other: "Who?"

"Well . . . ." She took his hands in hers and looked into his eyes. She lowered her voice: "You know about Sarah, right?"

He pretty much did now. He made a face. "No."

"I think you do."

"I didn't. But I think I get the idea."

She stroked one of his hands. "I'm sorry. I thought you knew about it. Are you angry with me?"

"No. Why don't you tell me? I've got a pretty good idea, but go ahead and tell me. Please."

"Oh, George. . . . I don't think I should."

That irritated him. "She's seeing another guy, right?"

She looked down melodramatically, still holding his hand. "I'm sorry. I've got a big mouth, huh?"

"Your mouth's fine. . . . You've got a beautiful mouth."

She acted surprised. "George . . . ." She stroked his hand again.

"You really think so?"

"Yes."

She looked down demurely. "Well, thank you." After a pause she said: "I'm really sorry I was the one to tell you. About Sarah."

George, quickly: "That's okay."

Terry, as if he hadn't said anything: "I mean, I just don't like to see my friend get hurt." She was still working his hand. He thought the situation was ridiculous, but he kept playing along. She continued: "I don't know what in the world got into Sarah anyway. Bobby Hawkins isn't anything. Why, I know there are a lot of girls who'd appreciate a guy like you." She paused.

George, still playing along: "Like who?"

Terry looked down, then eventually said, "Like . . . like me, maybe." She looked up shyly, then down again. He didn't say anything. She continued, "Gosh, here we are at the lake . . . ."

He wondered if she would take the initiative and kiss him if he waited long enough. Then he thought he was being a jerk about this. "Terry?"

"Yes?" She licked her lips. Her mouth parted a little.

"I'd like to kiss you."

She blinked. "Uh . . . well . . . ." She looked around. He wasn't supposed to ask; he was just supposed to do it. "I guess it would be okay. If you don't get the wrong idea."

"Okay." He put his arms around her and kissed her. Hugging her close, he felt her pointy bra boring into his chest a bit. He didn't mind. They made out for a while. At one point she actually started pushing him back. She backed him against the door, then realized what she'd done and pulled away, blushing. "Oh, excuse me." She looked down demurely again.

He said, "You're fine, sweetheart."

She smiled. " 'Sweetheart.' Wow. Are we going together now?"

"Uh . . . sure. I really like you."

She reached and squeezed his hand, keeping her eyes away. "I really like you too. . . . Everyone's going to say I took you away from Sarah . . . ."

He interrupted, saying dismissively, "Fuck 'em."

Her eyes widened. "What?"

"I mean, I don't care what they say. . . . Pardon me. I guess I don't like being played for a fool."

"Is that the only reason we're together tonight? So you can get even with Sarah?"

She was too much. The handlers should have sent her on their little odyssey. He said: "Of course not. I like being with you. I'm not thinking about Sarah."

Terry, demure: "Well . . . I like being with you too. . . . I wouldn't go out with someone who's already spoken for. That's not how I was brought up. But when I see Sarah going out with Bobby Hawkins . . . ."

"It's okay. I wasn't spoken for." Then he realized she could have made it all up about Hawkins. Or, more likely, Sarah and Hawkins had been together but it was totally or mostly innocent. On the other hand, he didn't care. "Okay?"

She looked up and gave him a shy smile. "Okay . . . sweetheart." He put his arms around her and pulled her close. She leaned into him and kissed him. They kissed for a while, like before. Then she leaned back into her seat, pulling him with her. He leaned into her. He reached for a lever or something to adjust the seat back, but couldn't find it. Then he felt her hand on the back of his; she guided his hand to a metal lever under the seat, and he pulled it. The seat flew back suddenly so it was completely horizontal. He laughed. She blushed, then gave a little laugh. "Oops. Here, I better fix it." She reached under the seat.

"Wait."

She hesitated. "What?"

"Well, this is sort of nice. I mean, it was awfully uncomfortable . . . ."

"Well . . . ."

He had to admire her. He kissed her. They put their arms around each other. After a while they leaned back, lying side by side. He could picture the business with the car seat in a show about the '50s made decades later, and it would be funny, but in a real '50s sitcom—which he was sure this was—this would be off camera. He was intrigued by her pointy breasts. He moved a hand gradually close to one of them, then cupped it gently. She suddenly grabbed his hand and moved it. In an angry whisper, she said, "No!"

"Excuse me."

"Well . . . I don't want you to get the wrong idea. I hope that's not why you came here."

"No. . . . I like kissing you though."

She smiled. They went back to what they'd been doing. He knew that to some extent he was playing the clown. So what? The handlers could laugh or react however they reacted.

He heard a "thump." Irritated, he said, "I don't believe it." Then he heard another "thump."

"What?"

"No big deal. Is there somewhere else we can go?"

"What's wrong with this place?" She put her hands gently on his neck. "What's wrong?"

He heard low voices. "I just think this place is going to weird out on us." He heard a car door slam, then another one.

The voices were louder now. Terry: " 'Weird out?' What are you talking about?"

He looked up. There were two wooden doors in frames behind her car, side by side about five feet apart. She'd have trouble backing out without hitting one or the other. A few people were milling around the doors. The couples in the other cars were stirring themselves to take an interest. It was sunset now. A guy looked over and said: "Hiya, George. Sarah."

George could imagine Terry's embarrassment. He said: "We broke up. I'm going with Terry now."

The guy looked surprised. "Terry?"

She sat up. "Hi," she said to the guy, waving, obviously hurt but trying to be brave.

"Hi," he responded, still stunned.

George, aggressive: "Got a problem with that, sport?"

"Hey, I'm your friend, George."

"Well, if you're my friend, you're Terry's friend."

People were milling around the doors. Guy: "Okay. Whatever you say." He walked on.

George turned to Terry. She was looking at him. She whispered, "Thank you." Then she hugged him and kissed him on the cheek.

They broke apart and looked at the others, all of whom were crowded around the doors now. Fairly quickly, the doors had taken everyone's mind off what they'd been doing. They knocked on the doors, walked around them, tried to open them, and talked about them. The women's makeup wasn't smeared; George reflected that it would have been in real life. George: "Now what?"

Terry: "What?"

"I'm wondering what to do."

"About the doors?" She looked closely at him; her makeup was a little smeared, but she didn't look funny to him. After a while, she said, "You know something about them, don't you?"

He nodded.

"What do you know?"

"It was déjà vu all over again."

"Huh? George, just tell me."

He whispered, "You really want to know?"

She whispered, "I really want to know."

He continued to whisper. "They lead to other worlds."

She laughed, then abruptly stopped. Then she was quiet a while, then she said, "That .... I don't understand."

A male voice said: "George! Terry! You've got to look at this!"

George, to Terry: "You open one, and you're looking at a whole other reality. Like maybe some old movie."

She watched the others. She said: "They can't open them. . . . Could you?"

"Yes."

She watched them a while longer. Someone else said, "Come on, you two, you've got to . . . ."

George held up a hand. "We'll be there. Just give us a minute."

Terry: "Why don't you open them?"

"I . . . I could. I don't really want to go to another world right now."

She narrowed her eyes. Eventually she asked, "Because of me?"

"Sort of."

"How do you know all this? You've lived here all your life, just like me."

"Not really."

"We've known each other since we were little kids."

"Maybe you've known me. But I haven't known you. The first time I saw you was when you pulled your car over to pick me up on the highway before."

A woman yelled, "How can you two . . . ?"

Terry, angrily: "Would you let us talk, please? We need to settle something! We don't care about your stupid doors!" To George, low voice again: "I just saw you this morning at school. You were coming out of the library. I was with Dorothy Adams. Remember?"

"No. I mean, I'm sure you saw me, and in a way it was me, but . . . I never experienced it. . . . I've never met Sarah."

"I don't understand. Could you just tell me what's going on."

"I'm from another world. Well . . . it's the United States, but it's the year 2000. . . ."

"This is crazy. You have a time machine?"

"Not exactly. . . ."

"I don't believe any of this. . . . I don't know how those doors got there, but this is crazy."

He shrugged. They were kicking the doors, to no avail.

Terry: "What would happen if you opened one of the doors?"

George thought about it. "You want . . . you want me to show you?"

"Will something bad happen?"

"Maybe. But I don't think so. . . . I can make sure nothing bad happens."

"Okay. Let's find out. . . . Hang on." She opened her purse, took out some tissues, and got to work fixing her make-up. When she was done she wiped a little lipstick off of him. "There. Let's go."

He turned around and stood up in the seat. "Folks, could I have your attention? Folks!" They stopped talking and moving and looked at him. "I think I can get those doors open, but I need everybody to stand back."

They looked at each other, then started to move away from the doors. The guy who had thought Terry was Sarah said: "Alright, George. They're all yours."

George said, "Thanks." He and Terry climbed out of her car, then held hands and approached the doors. He wished they were still making out. He made her stand back, then opened one of the doors. As he did he realized his sweatshirt had come off and was still in the car. The door opened toward him, as had all the others. On the other side was a beach filled with people in swimsuits from George's time, or close to that. The color got to him right away. It was a little intimidating, but he liked it. In the background was the ocean; a guy was parasailing, a woman was surfing. There was a volleyball game far to his right. At first he thought he was looking at the Xerxi commercial again, but no Xerxi was in sight. It all looked a little different anyway. There were fewer fun-in-the-sun activities. A guy behind him said, "Look at those girls!" There were appreciative murmurs from the other males. A woman said disapprovingly, "I can't believe they run around like that!" The other women murmured agreement. The swimsuits were more revealing than in the commercial; a few of the women wore thongs. That was the other big difference. George couldn't believe he'd noticed that last. The men on the beach tended to be muscular; the women tended to be curvaceous, with large breasts. Bad surf music came through the door, music that made the song Mickey played before seem like a masterpiece.

The '50s people made various comments; George didn't pay attention. A beach guy looked right at them. George waved. The guy waved back. Now George noticed two women wearing revealing latex science fiction sorts of outfits; both wore boots, one had thigh-high boots. A lot of the beach people were looking his way. The sci-fi women did the same. Now they, and a lot of other beach people, were walking toward the door. George: "Okay." He was tempted to just step through. But he didn't. He turned. "No one goes through this doorway. I mean it. Somebody tried that before with a different door and they died immediately." He walked back to Terry's car.

Terry, following him: "What *is* that? It's another world, isn't it?"

"Yes. It's closer to my time." The sweatshirt was on the floor of the front seat. He reached and grabbed it. "But it's not the real world. It's a bad movie." He needed to shut up. He tied the sweatshirt around his waist and started back. "Let's try that other door."

She stopped. "George?"

He stopped. The rest of them were captivated by the beach world. "What?"

"Is this a movie?"

She was pretty smart. "No." He wasn't lying.

"Then what is it?"

Should he tell her the truth? "It's a TV show."

She looked down, then gave a slow nod.

"I'm sorry."

She blurted, "Take me with you."

"I can't. I tried before—it killed the person I tried it with."

A guy by the doors called out: "Come on, Preston! Open the other door!"

George: "Sure."

Terry: "George?"

"Yes?"

"Can you stay here with me?"

It was one of the sweetest things anyone had ever said to him. After a few seconds, he said, "I don't think they'll let me." Even though he liked her, he also knew he didn't want to stay. He pushed that thought from his mind.

"Who won't let you?"

"I don't know."

She surprised him: "Well . . . fuck 'em."

"One time I just went to sleep and woke up in the next world. I'm sorry, Terry. I like you too."

Terry, unhappy, trying to take it all in: "Well . . . come on. I guess you better open that other door for them."

"I guess so." They rejoined the others. Guys were crowded around the open door. The two sci-fi women were on the other side; behind them were a bunch of beach guys. The '50s women looked annoyed. George could still hear surf music. The two groups were talking back and forth. He heard, "I love Earth men!" and "I can't believe you girls!" People on each side of the door tried to reach out over the threshold, but it didn't work. Someone would put his hand through, and it would disappear as it went through; then he'd pull it back and it would be fine. A '50s guy and one of the sci-fi women were pressing their palms together at the threshold, or trying to. George suspected they weren't actually touching, that to do so wasn't possible for them. He wondered why the '50s crowd wasn't more excited about seeing color. That was more striking to him than anything else.

A woman stood in front of him, fists on her hips. "Are you going to close that door?"

He stepped around her. "I think I'll open the other one." He walked up to it, told the few people near it to stand back, then pulled it open.

It was another black and white world. He was at the head of a huge dining table, with stuffy, well-dressed people eating and drinking. Servants moved quietly around the table carrying dishes and serving those who were seated. There were male and female diners and male and female servants. The hall was huge and elegant, with a very high ceiling. It all felt very British, and from a long time ago, maybe the '30s. The black and white was a different black and white. It was less sharp, somewhere between the Plucky O'Neill world and the one he was in. A few diners looked at him, then the conversation died away and they were all looking at him. A servant dropped a huge metal platter, which made a big resounding crash. George looked back; a crowd was gathering behind him, mostly female. They seemed curious and happy. He turned back to the dinner party. The closest diners were a formidable-looking middle-aged man with gray hair and a gray mustache, and, across from him, a hefty middle-aged woman with white hair and an imposing bosom. She was clearly too shocked to speak. The man raised a monocle to his eye, focused, and said, "Good Lord!" The other diners started to murmur.

George: "This isn't for me. Terry?" He turned to her, and stepped away from the door.

Terry: "What?"

The dinner party turned him off, but it crossed his mind again to enter the beach-bikini world. No. "Want to get out of here?"

She thought about it, then smiled. "I'd love to."

"Okay." He considered closing the doors but decided to let it go. There was some danger, but the right thing to do seemed to be to let them do what they wanted. He and Terry walked back to the car on the driver's side; he climbed in first and stepped across the seat to the passenger's side. She swung herself in after him, in a practiced, athletic motion he figured would have gotten a laugh from the viewers of a typical show. It would have looked slightly risqué. He asked, "Can you get us out?"

Brightly: "Of course I can." Some of the others reacted to their leaving—the gist of it was that they didn't want George to go since he apparently had some kind of power over the doors. He waved and said, "Gotta go." Terry was skillful behind the wheel. She pulled up and back a few times, angling the car, until she could back around the doors. She drove slow, and the others got out of their way, though a few persisted in asking them to stay. George said, "Have a good one, guys." Terry waved and said, "We'll see you later." Once she was past the crowd, she turned the car around, then started to take them back the way they'd come. She asked, "So where are we going?"

"I have no idea. Where do you want to go?"

"I don't know. Are we on a date?"

"Sure. It's . . . beyond a date."

She was silent a while. Then she said, "So what happens after you go?"

He thought about it. "I don't know." He didn't like thinking about it.

"I guess you wouldn't. I mean, you're always gone. How would you know?"

"Yeah. I . . . I'm sorry."

She was silent again, driving. Eventually, she asked, "So where should we go?"

He thought about that. He would have liked to just drive—get far away from the town, and not come back. However, if this world continued to exist after he left it, and the two of them had driven out of town together and he was never seen again, that wouldn't look good for her. How would she explain it? He doubted she'd be accused of murder, but it wouldn't be good. Maybe "George" the sitcom character would still be around, just like he had been around in the sitcom's past. But should George count on that? He didn't want to see his sitcom family again, but there didn't seem to be another way to do right by her than to go back to them. There was a good chance he'd wake up somewhere else—he'd never stayed in one world very long. On the other hand, he could leave town with her if she approved, then make any downside up to her by giving her a list of companies she should invest in in the future. Of course, what the future held for this sitcom world was uncertain—maybe the same companies wouldn't hit it big. And he didn't like the idea anyway—it seemed like bullshit. He asked, "Is there somewhere else on the lake we can go?"

"Maybe." She continued to the highway and turned onto it so they were headed the way they'd been headed before. She asked, "You don't know your way around, do you?"

"No."

"That's okay." After a couple of minutes she turned off the highway and followed a road to a college campus, where he assumed they were students. It was completely dark and quiet. She took them through the campus and then to a road which she followed to the opposite side of the lake from the place where they'd been, to a smaller and, obviously, lesser-known spot. She turned off the car, and asked, "Is this a good place?"

"It's beautiful." He remembered something he needed to settle. "Uh . . . did you see through the first doorway?"

"Of course."

"See anything strange?"

"Yes. . . . It was all strange. Why?"

"Do you know what color is?"

"Of course."

That didn't make sense. Then he got it. "You see color all around you, don't you?"

"Sure. Don't you?"

"No. Since I've been here all I've seen is black and white."

"Like a TV show?"

"Yeah."

"I'm sorry."

"Don't be. I was just curious. . . . I . . . uh . . . I'd like to kiss you some more."

She smiled. "Well . . . you have my permission." He kissed her. They made out. After a few minutes, she reached under the seat and touched a lever, and the seat popped back. They lay down side by side, still kissing. He liked it, and eventually got very turned-on, but he didn't try to go further. Eventually, she said, "Well, I guess we better be heading back."

"Yeah, I know." She drove him back to his parents' house.

On the way he asked her, "Terry?"

"Yes?"

"What was I like . . . what was I like before you picked me up tonight? In all the years you knew George before tonight?"

She thought. "Because that wasn't you, right?"

"Right."

"Well . . . George was a lot like you. He was just like you, a real nice guy, but he knew his way around . . . and he fit in more."

"Thanks. Just curious."

"And he never would have gone out with me."

He didn't know what to say. "I'm sorry." Then he added, "That's his loss."

"It's okay."

"I'm glad I ran into you tonight."

She smiled. "Me too."

In front of the house, he kissed her and held her, and they said goodnight. He felt very attached to her and didn't think he'd see her again, but he didn't want a big goodbye scene. Apparently she felt the same way.

He walked up the sidewalk to the house. The front door was unlocked. He went inside, thinking his father would be up and would initiate an unpleasant conversation, and he was right about both. His father, wearing pajamas and a robe, reading the paper, drinking a glass of milk, asked, "Where were you, Son?"

George felt newly insulted by the pretense that this guy was his father. He didn't particularly have anything against the guy. It was the principle of the thing. "I was with Terry Cannutto."

The dad was confused. "*Terry Cannutto?* Well, what were you two doing?"

"We were on a date."

"Date? Well . . . what about Sarah Woods? She called tonight."

"Things didn't work out with us. I like Terry an awful lot. We've known each other a long time, you know."

He sounded even more befuddled. "Well . . . Son, I . . . . Terry's a nice girl; I just . . . . Well, are you sure she's right for you? That . . . you two are right for each other?"

"No. But I think she's a great gal, and I want to give it a shot. I better go to bed. Good night." He started up the stairs, taking them two at a time.

Unhappy: "Good night."

George went to the bathroom to piss, then went to his room. He tossed the overnight bag or whatever it was on the floor and dropped *Captured* on top of it, then took the sweatshirt from around his waist and put it on the right way. He didn't want to risk having it come off while he tossed and turned, since that could mean losing it if they threw him into another world. Then he hit the light and lay down. He was fully clothed—he even kept his shoes on. It took him a while to fall asleep.

## CHAPTER 11

George felt a jolt from below and woke up. The world was in color again. He was sitting in the back seat of a car. It was night. Next to him was Benny Moriarty, the director of a bunch of hip crime thrillers. The guy dabbled in acting and played small roles in all of his movies. In the front seat, behind the wheel, was a large black man with, remarkably, an afro. The black man was smoking a cigar; Moriarty was smoking a cigarette. The smell of smoke, especially from the cigar, was heavy, but George didn't mind. They were driving through an alley in a city. The car was huge. The seats were black vinyl. Between George and Moriarty was a red shoebox with string tied around it. Probably important to the story, but not to George. He liked the car, which wouldn't have been too out of place in the last world. It might date from the '60s. The first time he'd ever seen a Moriarty film he'd been spellbound. It was *Bad Dudes*, which he'd seen on video. As soon as it was over he'd rewound it and watched it again from start to finish. But his opinion of Moriarty and his films had declined steadily since then.

The car stopped abruptly next to a nondescript metal door. The black man got out, unhurried, straightened his jacket—which was red leather but cut like a suit jacket, and he wore it buttoned—, went around the car to the metal door, knocked on it a couple of times, then got back in the car on the passenger's side. He was Robert Smith, an actor who appeared in most of Moriarty's films. The metal door opened, and Sullok came out. His hair was in a ponytail, and he wore jeans and a black leather jacket. He closed the door behind him, walked around the car, and got in the driver's seat.

Smith said, in a deep voice: "Now, I want to clarify my point here. I'm not saying I wouldn't go out with a redhead. I'm saying every fuckin' redhead I ever knew was a fuckin' psycho. I mean, not right away. They'll be cool for a while. But sooner or later man, they fuckin' blow. And you do *not* want to be around when that happens."

Sullok took out a cigarette and lit it.

Moriarty: "So how many redheaded women you know?"

Smith: "Man, I don't know *any* redheads. That was my goddam point. I don't need that shit."

Moriarty: "So how do you know this?"

"Well I have *known* some in the fuckin' past."

"So you ever fucked any?"

Slightly irritated: "A few. Nothing wrong with 'em that way. Quite the fuckin' contrary. It's when you stick around after the show—that's when you have to pay."

"So would you fuck Lizzie Jones?"

"*Lizzie Jones?* Where the fuck you get that shit? Why the hell would you ask me that?"

"I'm just asking. You don't think she's attractive?"

Still surprised at the question: "She's got to be in her goddam sixties by now."

"No shit she's old now. I mean when she did her show."

"I never thought about it."

Sullok: "I think she was hot."

Moriarty: "How 'bout you George?"

George slowly shook his head, not in answer to the question but in a general reaction to his environment.

Moriarty: "You don't like her?"

George didn't say anything.

Smith: "Is that what you fuckin' white boys do? You sit around watchin' reruns of the fuckin' *Lizzie Jones Show* and jerk off."

Moriarty: "You got a problem with that?"

Smith laughed. "Hey, you know, I just want to understand white culture."

They all laughed, including George. Moriarty: "So George. You're not gonna stick up for Lizzie. I mean, she's a sister redhead isn't she?"

George still didn't talk.

"I asked you a question."

No answer.

"Hey, you have a nice nap?" He reached for George's shoulder.

George held a hand up. "Don't you fucking touch me!"

Moriarty took his hand back. "Okay. Fuck you."

George thought about saying "Fuck you," but that would be lame. He said, "Maybe if I keep repeating 'fuck' and 'nigger' enough nobody'll know I can't write."

No one said anything for a few seconds. Then Moriarty: "What the hell are you talking about?"

George rolled his eyes.

"Don't you roll your fucking eyes at me."

Smith, angry: "Hey, would you both shut the fuck up!"

George, to Smith: "You're an ass."

Smith, turning around and kneeling on his seat, his voice relatively calm: "Excuse me. What the fuck . . . ? Hey, pull this goddam car over."

George, deepening his voice: "Don't make me come back there!"

Smith: "Hey, you makin' fun of me, nigga? You a fuckin' redheaded dead man, mothafucka!" To Sullok, but still watching George: "Pull this mothafuckin' car over!"

Sullok, still driving, put out his cigarette, then drew a fairly large gun out of his jacket and pointed it at Smith. "Shut the fuck up, Joseph. I'm pointing a gun at your goddam head. I'm not kidding."

Joseph, turning around and sitting: "Yeah, fuck you too, mothafucka. Red, I fuckin' owe you one. That goes for you too, Stevie."

George: "How 'bout we pull over?"

Sullok: "George, could you show a little restraint here?"

George: "This is a fucking joke, Sullok. It was cute for a while . . ."

Moriarty, exasperated: "What the fuck are you talking about?"

George felt a little irritation with himself for having said anything at all, let alone talking to Sullok. But nobody was perfect. He was silent again.

Moriarty: "What the fuck . . . ? Can you fucking hear me?"

Sullok: "Shut up Nate."

Nate, sullen: "Yeah, fuck you."

They sat in silence for a while.

George: "Hey, could you guys turn on the radio?"

Joseph: "George, at this moment, I am reminded of a scene from *The Thesiad*. Have you read *The Thesiad*?"

George, after a pause: "So, how about the radio?"

Joseph, slowly and dramatically: "There is a scene in which the great hero Alantyl looks over the battlefield early in the morning. He sees the opposing army, a mighty gathering of warriors. And he calls out to them: 'The invincible Alantyl shall make meat of you all! He shall leave you as bone and blood! Come war!' " He was yelling by the end.

There was a silence. Then George: "I don't think that's in *The Thesiad*."

Joseph quickly turned around and kneeled on the seat again, and pulled out a large silver gun. He said in a singsong, mocking voice, "Hey there, nigga, my dick is big, but my gun is bigga!" He pointed the gun at George's face. "You want to die, mothafucka? Why don't you say one more mothafuckin' word?"

George stared at him. The car screeched to a halt. George: "Maybe if I honk enough about what a badass I am and kill enough unarmed people, then I'll be a man." He hadn't expected to finish the sentence.

Sullok: "I'm pointing a gun at your motherfucking head, Joseph. You goddam twitch and I'll blow you the fuck away. You hear me?"

Joseph: "Fuck you, man!"

"Okay. I know you can probably take George with you. I don't care. You open your fucking mouth again, I'm gonna blow a tunnel in your head. I fucking mean it." He paused. Joseph clenched his jaw muscles, looking with hatred at George. "You want to swing around? Try to shoot me? Make your move." The jaw muscles were still clenched, and Joseph quivered with rage, but he said nothing. "Okay. I want you to hand George your gun."

Joseph: "Say what?" Sullok fired. Joseph's head seemed to explode. Gore and bone fragments went everywhere; George was hit hard by it.

George, as he wiped gore away from his closed eyes. "Thank you."

Nate: "What the fuck . . . ? I don't believe this shit!"

George looked on the floor. There, with plenty of blood on it, was Joseph's gun.

Sullok kneeled on the seat to face George and Nate. "Nate. Shut up."

"What, you gonna kill me too?"

"No. I'm just saying get yourself under control. Could you do that please?"

George picked up the gun and pointed it at Sullok's face. Sullok didn't move or say anything. His face showed just a little surprise.

Nate: "What the fuck are you doing?"

George shot Sullok between the eyes. There was another gory explosion.

## CHAPTER 12

George was sitting behind a wooden desk in what looked like a sheriff's office in a Western. It was hot. There was a jail cell in the room, empty. Through a couple of windows he could see people walking around in Western garb. He looked at himself. None of the gore from Sullok's violent death had reached him, but he was still a mess from Joseph. Sitting on the desk were a tin star and a cowboy hat. The bloody silver gun was still in his hand. He set it on the desk and stood up. His sweatshirt had quite a bit of blood on it, most of it fresh, and there was blood on his jeans as well. There was also solid matter from Smith still on him. He found a waste can and brushed the solid stuff into it. It crossed his mind that this stuff was partly brain, and some of it was obviously bone. He did his best to stop thinking about it. For a few moments he thought he might vomit, but the feeling went away.

His skin felt damp from blood. He took the sweatshirt off. A lot of blood had soaked through to his shirt, which he now saw was light blue. He put the sweatshirt back on. A door opened; he looked up. Sullok walked in, wearing cowboy hat, boots, vest, button shirt, tan pants, tin star, and a ponytail. Sullok: "Well, how you doin', Sheriff?"

"I'm okay."

"How . . . what happened to you?"

George didn't feel the need at the moment to give him the silent treatment, but he didn't want to talk at length with the man. "Got in a fight."

Sullok laughed. "Looks like a fight involving a bullet or two."

George walked back to the desk. "Two." He tapped on the tin star. "If I'm Sheriff I formally resign. See ya." He picked up the silver gun. Then he noticed a gun belt with a wooden-handled six shooter in it hanging on a coat rack by the door. The belt held a lot of bullets for reloading. He pointed and asked, "Is that mine?"

Sullok nodded.

He flicked on the safety of the silver gun and stuck it in the waistband of his jeans—it didn't really fit, but he'd have to deal with it. He walked over to the gun belt and put it on. Sullok walked to the desk and sat behind it. He picked up the star and looked at it with mild curiosity.

George: "Thanks for saving my life."

"My pleasure." He could have saved George's life in the preceding story in this world, of course.

George looked around to see if there was anything else he wanted. He considered the cowboy hat—it was sunny out—but decided to let it go. Not his style. He said, "See ya later."

"See ya."

George walked out into the street. He squinted into the sun. However, though it was hot, the air was dry. Very different from Unionville in the summer. Everyone looked at him; a few people stopped in their tracks to do so. People murmured. He frowned and started walking faster. Then he slowed down. He wanted to get to his house, but he didn't know where it was. He passed by a slender middle-aged woman; she looked at him with mild fear and puzzlement and said, "Sheriff...."

He stopped. "Do you know where I live?"

Even more puzzled: "Yes.... The hotel."

Why was he living in a hotel? Maybe he hadn't been Sheriff long. "Which way?"

She blinked, then slowly pointed over his right shoulder.

He turned. There was a building, nicer than the rest, with a wooden sign reading "Hotel" hanging in front of it. He said, "Thank you," and headed that way.

"You're welcome."

He could take the sweatshirt off but that wouldn't help much. At least the sweatshirt was dark. The sneakers would look pretty odd here, but he doubted people were paying much attention to his feet.

A tall guy with sideburns approached him and said, "What the hell happened to you, Sheriff?"

George, still moving: "Got in a fight." The guy gave a big laugh. George didn't want to talk to him or any of them. Whoever was picking these places was racking up very low scores for originality. The Benny Moriarty wasn't as clichéd a choice, at least. But the choice of this world was absurdly obvious. He'd liked Westerns when he was a kid, but he didn't like them much now. He liked the action, but not much else. He hated the machismo.

He entered the hotel. The lobby was pretty fancy, with plush, wine-colored furniture. There was a wooden counter with a clerk behind it, a

## ADVENTURE

young man in spectacles who looked like a bookworm—what George was in real life. Behind the clerk were rows of wooden boxed openings, each of which had a number carved above it. On the counter was a call bell. George approached the guy, who said brightly: "Hello, Sheriff Preston. I've got a telegram for you." He turned around, grabbed a piece of paper from an opening with the number 14 above it, and handed it to George.

George accepted it. "Which way to my room, please?"

The clerk frowned and shook his head. "Are you playing with me, Sheriff?"

George, in a no-nonsense tone: "No. Which way to my room, please?"

"Right up the stairs. . . . Anything else, sir?"

"No. Thank you." George walked toward the steps, looking at the telegram. It read: "We'll be seeing you. W. M." He shoved it in his pocket.

At the top of the stairs was a nicely carpeted hallway, near the end of which he found Room 14. It was locked. Of course he didn't have the key. "Shit."

He went back down the hall, then down the stairs and into the lobby. There he saw a big, heavy guy with a black beard and mustache slapping the clerk. The man had his hand on the clerk's collar; he'd pulled the clerk's head halfway across the counter. The clerk was wide-eyed with fear. The man turned to George and smiled amiably. "Howdy." Still smiling at George, he backhanded the clerk.

George especially hated the scenes in Westerns in which the bookish characters were physically abused by the he-men, both villains and heroes. He pulled up his sweatshirt, took out the silver gun, which still had blood on it, and pointed it at the big man. The man's smile went away, replaced, of course, by a look of confusion. He let go of the clerk, who took a breath, backed away from the counter, and straightened his shirt. He looked a little less fearful now. The big man said, "What in the hell's gotten into you?"

George approached him, still pointing the gun. "Why'd you hit that man?"

The big man smiled again, looked at the clerk, then looked back. "Oh, that. . . . Well, why not?"

George stopped a couple of yards away from the man. He remembered the safety was on and flicked it off. "Is that your answer?"

The man stopped smiling again, and started to look angry. "I don't like this."

"I didn't ask if you did. I asked about the clerk."

"Well, alright. I asked what room you was in and he wouldn't tell me."

"No shit he wouldn't tell you. He's not supposed to tell you."

"Well, maybe I don't like some half-man who shuffles papers for a

111

living who won't answer a question when I ask it."

George imagined the big man was a "good guy." The viewers or readers were probably supposed to find him likably gruff and hearty.

"There's more than one kind of man, hoss. You would have thought he was a weakling if he *had* told you the room."

The man appeared to think about it. "So you're on his side?"

George thought for a few seconds himself. It wasn't about who was right; it was about what was right. But he saw no point in saying that. He said, "Yes."

"I won't take this."

"But the clerk was supposed to take being slapped around."

"To hell with him."

The clerk, fear in his voice: "To hell with you, Mister."

The man turned and said, "Boy, you talk awfully . . ."

George yelled, "Shut the fuck up!"

The man turned his head back to George; his eyes blazed with anger. "You want to be half a man, put that goddam gun down and fight like one."

"I'm not half a man, and I don't have to prove a goddam thing. You'd win the fight, and you'd still be an asshole."

The man was furious. Teeth clenched: "Nobody talks to me like that. Not even you. I don't know what's gotten into you, but as soon as the McCawley brothers are taken care of, there's gonna be a reckonin'."

George thought about that. "That's fine. Until then we got a truce. Deal?"

The man gave a tight, hostile smile, and said sarcastically, "That's fine."

"That means a truce regarding the clerk, too. You don't touch him or talk to him until the McCawleys are gone. Fair enough?"

Again sarcastically: "That's fine."

George flicked the safety on, put the gun back in his jeans, and walked away. The clerk said, "Thank you, Sheriff."

George turned to face them both. The big man stared hatefully at him. To the clerk he said: "You're welcome. But I'm not the sheriff. I resigned." He turned again and resumed walking.

Behind him George heard the big man say: "Remember, George. A reckonin'." George walked out of the hotel. The townspeople still stared at his sweatshirt; at least no one else said anything about it. He went back to the sheriff's office, where Sullok was sitting at the desk, reading a book.

Sullok, looking up briefly and nodding: "George."

George: "Sullok. I mean . . . hi." He looked around for keys, and didn't see any.

Sullok laughed. "Okay. Sullok to you too."

# ADVENTURE

George walked over to the desk and said, "Excuse me." Sullok scooted the chair back, picking up the book. George checked the top drawer—among letters, a bandana, and other things that didn't interest him, he saw one largish metal ring with several keys on it, and another ring with a single key. He took out both rings.

Sullok, extending his hand: "Can't let you have those, hoss." He reached and, politely, took just the ring with multiple keys. "I'm more or less the acting sheriff right now."

"Sure." George wanted to ask if the key he still had was for his hotel room—he'd feel very stupid walking back again. But he'd rather do that than ask. He kept his mouth shut. Now that he thought about it, he wouldn't come back, either, even if this wasn't the right key. He didn't need the hotel room. He glanced around the sheriff's office to see if there was anything else he wanted. There was a rifle leaning in a corner. He knew enough about Westerns to know that would be his best ticket in a gunfight. But he let it go. He didn't want to carry it around, and losing a gunfight wouldn't matter much. He started to leave.

Sullok: "Have you ever thought about where you'd like to go?"

George looked back over his shoulder. Sullok was scooting back to the desk and placing the open book on it. He was looking at the book, like he was reading. George: "I'd like to go home."

Still looking down: "Where's home?"

"Sawyerville, Illinois."

"You sure?"

"Yep." He walked out. If Sullok meant was he sure Sawyerville was home, it was a dumb thing to ask. Unionville was more home to him, but he wanted to return to Sawyerville, where his life was, and if Sullok was doing some kind of speculating about the true meaning of home, George wanted no part of it. If Sullok meant was he sure he wanted to stop whatever all this was and get back to his life, he wasn't sure. His real-life future hadn't been shaping up to be great. And after these worlds, even a pretty interesting life might seem like one long anticlimax. But whatever he did in his life, it would be real. If his future wasn't shaping up to be great, maybe he could make some choices and make it better. This roller coaster was pointless. Or maybe it wasn't pointless, but it was a bullshit deal as far as he was concerned. Furthermore, he'd said a long time ago that he wanted to go home and he'd meant it to be final. And they'd jerked him around repeatedly, as far as he was concerned. Besides that, he'd already had his fun, such as it was. He'd liked some of the worlds, and he'd gotten something, at least, out of each of them. He was ready to go back to his life, for better or worse, and he'd try not to look back. It occurred to him that he might go from world to world indefinitely. He immediately stopped thinking about that.

A few people spoke to him as he walked back to the hotel; he more or less ignored them. As he entered the hotel lobby the clerk looked up, nodded smartly, and said, "Mr. Preston."

George said, "Hello," and then nodded. He went to the room and tried the key, and was relieved that it worked. He went in and closed and locked the door behind him. It was a good-sized room, almost as nice as the rest of the hotel. The furniture looked expensive and comfortable, though the room didn't quite have the decadent look of the lobby. There was a newspaper, a few books, and some clothes lying on a chair, on the bed, and on the floor. He tossed the key on the bed. He opened a dresser drawer and saw old-fashioned underwear; he opened another and saw shirts. The problem would be getting the sweatshirt home. Then he wondered why he needed to get it home. Screw it. It hadn't been particularly important to him before. It would be a souvenir of his adventure if he got it back, but that would be true of whatever he happened to be wearing when he got back. Of course, the sweatshirt had the tears front and back from a spear, a sword, and a gunshot. That was special, but you couldn't have everything. He'd gone to quite a bit of trouble so far to hang on to it, but that would be a dumb reason to go to a lot more trouble. He took off the sweatshirt and dropped it on the floor, then did the same with the '50's sitcom shirt. His stomach had some dried blood on it. He could live with that. He picked out a green button shirt and put it on. It fit perfectly; he'd have been surprised if it hadn't. His jeans also had blood on them. He switched them for another pair. The new pair was a little less comfortable, but that wasn't a big deal. He noticed a pair of black cowboy boots at the foot of the bed, and went over to try them on. He had difficulty getting them on, but once on they were surprisingly comfortable. He tucked his jeans into them. He walked around the room, which was a bit tricky, given the high heels. He smiled. He liked them; among other things he liked the shining metal toes. But in his own eyes he seemed like a buffoon in them. He had a friend who occasionally wore cowboy boots, and on a lot of people they looked great. But he wasn't one of those people. He took them off—which was even more difficult than putting them on—and put his sneakers back on, feeling like he was trading down.

He went through the room to see if there was anything else he wanted. The newspaper told him it was May 20, 1871, or close to that, anyway, and that this was Chance, Texas. In a drawer he found a short stack of alien-looking paper bills. It hadn't even occurred to him that the money he'd come with was useless here. He took his wallet out and looked at his money, including his change. The dime sported the face of a president who hadn't been born yet. He folded the 1871 money in half and put it in the pocket that didn't already have money in it. He took a red bandana out of the same drawer, folded it, and put it in the same pocket. One top of the dresser he saw a round pocket watch, without a chain. He opened it—the time was, roughly, 1:12 in the afternoon. He closed the watch and put it in his shirt pocket. An image crossed his mind of the watch stopping a bullet, and he laughed.

What did he want to do? He was getting hungry—he could start by going somewhere and having a steak. But then what? It was almost a point of honor by now to walk away from whatever world he was in, unless he was somehow being entertained. He wasn't being entertained here. But he'd probably be walking into another desert or something not far removed from it. He'd be on foot in a world where people traveled on horseback or by carriage or rail. Of course he could buy a horse. In fact, he probably already owned one—they could show him where it was and treat him to more puzzled looks. He'd only been riding once in his life, at a summer camp, but nevertheless he thought he could probably ride well enough to get by. But he'd also have to camp out, which would mean supplying himself beforehand, and would generally be a pain in the ass. Or he could commit suicide by blowing his brains out. But that seemed very wrong. He didn't know for a fact that it wouldn't be final, but that wasn't it. He didn't know for a fact that any kind of death in one of these worlds wouldn't be final, but he wasn't much worried about that anymore. Suicide as a convenient way of jumping worlds just wasn't for him. He could simply walk out of the town and let the world do its worst. If things got bad enough, he could take his own life after all. He didn't like the idea, but he'd take it over dying of exposure in a desert. Probably, it wouldn't be long anyway before he was in the next world. Or he could take a stagecoach or train out of town, which would require hanging around the town a while, he supposed about a day. Screw that. He would walk out.

He put the silver gun back in the front of his jeans, thought it looked stupid, took it out, and set it on the dresser. He was parting with the one advantage he would have had in a potential gunfight, but that was okay. He left the room—he considered getting the key and locking the door behind him, and decided not to. His conscience nagged him a little about that, briefly, in spite of everything. In the lobby, he asked the clerk for the best place in town to get a steak. The clerk—thoughtful enough to mask his surprise at the question—directed him to a restaurant a few buildings down on the other side of the street. George thanked him and headed that way. Of course, they had a story ready for him, as in most of these worlds. This one apparently involved a climactic gunfight with the McCawleys. If that actually happened, it would be in spite of George. Yet this wasn't likely to surprise the handlers. In their shoes, he would be surprised if he, George as subject or whatever, *did* play along with the scenario. He could do so this time just to screw with them, but he didn't want to bother.

Perhaps because he looked preoccupied, no one spoke to him as he walked to the restaurant. Inside, a man with a thick black mustache and red bands on his shirtsleeves took George's order, for a steak and a beer. The service was relatively fast, and the large steak came with a similarly large baked potato. They tasted better than he imagined they would have in a real Western town of the era. The beer came in a big glass mug. While he was eating, someone sat down across from him. George winced, then sighed, then looked up. The guy was slightly bigger than George, clean-shaven, light brown hair. He took off his cowboy hat. He was going to lay a lot of guilt on George about leaving the town in its hour of need. He said, in greeting, "George."

"Hi. Can I get you a steak? Maybe a beer?"

"I . . . uh . . . I don't think so." He had a concerned look.

George set his knife and fork down. Irritated: "Can I help you?"

Uncomfortable: "Can you . . . ? Well, Sam Green said you was steppin' down as Sheriff." He looked George in the eye. "I can't believe that."

George held the other man's gaze. "It's true. I'm gonna finish my steak now." He picked up his knife and fork and returned his attention to his food. Guilty feelings welled up.

The guy slowly stood up. "It's just . . . I never took you for a coward."

George looked up, furious. He knew that the word "coward" was a supreme insult in these stories. His mouth was full of food; he spat it on the floor. "I'm no coward, asshole. I just don't want to play anymore." He stood up. "And now that I think about it, the one thing I hate the most in these fucking worlds is the guilt people keep laying on me. I hate the goddam guilt worse than anything." He wasn't hungry anymore; he just wanted to get away. He took the Old West money out of his pocket, started to grab some of the bills, and then dropped all of them on the table. Then he picked up the glass of beer and hurled it with a crash on the wooden floor.

The man just sat there. As George walked away the man said, "I don't know you."

George didn't respond. He walked out of the restaurant and into the middle of the street, and kept walking. He had been planning to go to a saloon, just to see it, but fuck that. He could see where the street and the town ended, not far from him. He heard someone yell, "Coward!"

He turned. "Who said that?"

The man who'd slapped the clerk stepped away from a small group of people near the hotel and said: "I did. . . . Who are we going to fight, George? Are we going to fight each other or the McCawleys?"

"I'm no coward. I don't . . . ."

"Then prove it! Hell, I know you're not a coward. I just want you to show me, show us all tonight when they ride in. Let's fight 'em together!"

"No. . . . Good luck against them. I hope you win." He turned around and walked. Did he put up with shit, not respond to a great insult? Well, fuck that, anyway. It was all part of their game. None of the people on the street said anything else to him. It occurred to him that he could have done this, just walked away, the minute he appeared in this world. Well, so he was an idiot. So what?

Just after he passed the last building, he heard a "thump," and saw a wooden door in a frame appear a few yards in front of him. He stopped in front of it, turned the knob, and pulled it open.

He was looking into a cartoon world. He saw a gray stone floor, beyond which was a wall topped by a battlement, far below which he could see lush green hills. Beyond them was forest. The sky, in contrast to the appealing look of the countryside, was gray. The animation wasn't good. He suspected he was looking at the top of a castle or some other kind of fortress. Close enough. He walked through the doorway.

## CHAPTER 13

George didn't bother turning around—he knew the doorway had silently vanished. He looked only briefly at his own body, which was now of course bad animation like everything else. This roof or whatever you'd call it was square, maybe forty yards by forty yards. He walked to the nearest battlement and looked down. There was a moat. He was on top of a castle. He turned to look for a way down into it. In the corners were raised battle platforms, circular in shape. He walked toward the nearest one. He couldn't hear his own footsteps. He stopped. He couldn't hear anything. He snapped his fingers. No sound. He shrugged and continued to the platform. There was a trapdoor in the floor. He tried to open it but couldn't.

He started for the next platform. He heard something to his right and looked that way. A trapdoor had opened in the platform that was diagonal to the one he'd just been on; a green and brown creature emerged from it, a kind of lizard-man, climbing upward as if via a ladder. The creature wore a red loincloth and carried a spiked club. George heard its heavy breathing. It walked toward him. It had a big tail and sharp teeth, and it seemed to be smiling. He took out his revolver and pointed it at the creature's face. He tried to say, 'Stop!' but no sound came out. He fired over its head. He heard the shot—it wasn't terribly loud. The creature did not react at all; it simply kept coming. Behind it he saw Sullok climbing up through the trapdoor. Sullok wore a bright green robe, with a gold chain for a belt. Around his neck was a blue gem on a thin gold chain. His blond hair, for the first time in a long time, was not in a ponytail. His face was expressionless. George wouldn't have had a good shot at him, and didn't care to shoot him at the moment anyway. He calmly pulled the hammer back on the revolver with his free hand and fired again, this time at the creature's face. The bullet hit the creature's neck with a red flash and a ricochet sound. There was no apparent damage, and no reaction by the creature. This was obviously one of those first-person computer games where you killed huge quantities of monsters. But not with a six shooter from a Western. The creature had covered about half the distance between them. He moved backward quickly, still calm, pulled the hammer back and fired again, this time at the creature's right eye. The bullet hit its snout and bounced away. Sullok was walking behind it. George had been kidding himself aiming at the eye—the program wouldn't be detailed enough to make the eyes vulnerable.

He wasn't particularly mad at Sullok now, but Sullok and the creature were both coming after him. He was supposed to fight them in this world, and he was certainly going to defend himself. Sullok was fair game. He couldn't seem to damage the creature but maybe he could damage Sullok. He ran in an arc to get a better angle on the man. Running, he could hear his feet and his breathing. The creature, slow but with much less ground to cover, moved in an arc to match him, putting Sullok behind itself again. George tried to say, "Shit!" but again no sound came out. He had a decent shot at Sullok anyway, since Sullok was almost a head taller than the broad, squat creature. He pulled back the hammer and fired at Sullok's face, and missed. Sullok didn't react. George pulled back the hammer again, held the gun with both hands, and fired again. He saw a green flash a little to the side of Sullok's face, and heard a ricochet sound. Sullok still didn't react. George tried again. There was a green flash in front of Sullok's cheek, the ricochet sound, no apparent damage, and no reaction. Sullok and the creature had been advancing steadily all the while, but were still a fair distance away. George mouthed the question, "Did I fire six shots or only five?" Sullok smiled.

They were about 15 yards away. George had a clear path to the platform from which they'd emerged; he ran to that platform and tried the trapdoor. It wouldn't open. He hadn't noticed it closing. He looked up at his pursuers. They were now about 20 yards away, moving at the same speed. He could seemingly avoid them forever, or at least until he got tired. He jogged to another platform. There was no trapdoor. They had turned to follow him, but had covered little ground. The noises made by the creature hadn't varied. It breathed heavily, and every so often it roared. It seemed to bounce as it advanced. Sullok made no sound. He bounced as well, but only slightly—he was more dignified about it. George ran around them to the platform he hadn't tried. There was no trapdoor there. That was it. He looked over the battlement. He guessed that he was the equivalent of about five stories high. He wasn't going to jump. It was high enough to kill him, but not right away. Unfortunately, the lizard-man would, if it got close enough, also kill him, but not right away.

He tried Sullok again with the revolver; it was empty. He stayed away from them, which was easy, and reloaded. This was a pain—he pushed the cylinder out, pulled a bullet out of his belt, slid it into the cylinder, and repeated. When he was finished he pushed the cylinder back in place, hearing it click. He then unloaded all six shots into the creature's face, a couple at pretty close range, all to no effect. He reloaded again, and fired six shots at Sullok. He hit the creature twice and missed both of them once. His other three shots were on-target but simply bounced off the shield. At least, he assumed Sullok was protected by some kind of magic shield—it wouldn't make any sense for him to be naturally impervious to bullets. George then tried to run around them to get a shot at Sullok's back, or at least his side, but even running his hardest he couldn't get around them faster than Sullok and the creature, not hurrying, could turn. This was pointless, as well as irritating. He ran to one of the platforms and fired several shots at its trapdoor. He got noise and red flashes but did no damage. He reloaded yet again. He'd gone through more than half of his bullets.

He climbed onto the platform's battlement and jumped, hoping to reach the moat. If he didn't think he was going to make it he would shoot himself in the head in mid-air. He looked down, falling fast, hearing a kind of wind noise, and saw to his surprise that he was in fact going to hit the moat. Then he slammed into the cold water, and was submerged. Smiling, underwater, he let go of the gun, swam to the surface, and continued swimming to the far side. He pulled himself out of the water and heard a fizzing sound behind him. He turned and saw the water surface foam and bubble, then saw evil-looking little fish with open mouths and tiny sharp teeth jumping in small arcs above the water. He noticed water was dripping off of him, and then he was completely dry. That surprised him for a moment, but it made sense. The game wouldn't have you walking around for any length of time dripping water. He couldn't resist looking back up at the castle. The creature stood behind a battlement, looking at him. Behind it, still, was Sullok. George, laughing silently, waved. Sullok waved back.

George turned and walked away from the castle. He hadn't been walking a full minute when a wooden door in a frame appeared maybe ten feet in front of him, with, of course, a "thump." He walked up to it, turned the knob, and pulled it open.

It was a black and white world, the black and white a little less sharp than that of the '50s world. He was looking into some kind of office. A few feet away was another door, consisting mostly of a large pebble glass pane with the word "PRIVATE" on it in reverse letters. There was a small old-fashioned lamp on a small wooden table by the door. The walls were light gray, and bare except for a calendar. He could see a trench coat hanging in a corner. Well, it beat the computer game. He stepped through.

## CHAPTER 14

George stopped and looked around, taking care not to look back over his shoulder right away. The trench coat was on a coat rack that also had a hat on it. The room had, besides what he'd seen through the doorway, a bookshelf, a filing cabinet, a large wooden table with books and papers on it, a black leather armchair in a corner, and a cluttered wooden desk by a window. One of the items on the desk was a snub-nosed gun. The window was covered by a thin curtain, through which he could see it was day. Behind the desk was a wooden swivel chair. The floor was bare wood.

He wondered what to do. He walked to the window and looked out—he was in a city again, a few stories up. On the street were big, boxy cars, men in suits, coats or raincoats, and hats, and women in dresses, coats or raincoats, and, with a few exceptions, hats. It wasn't raining, but it had been recently. He turned away from the window.

The door opened. A blond woman, mid thirties, wearing a blouse, a jacket, and a knee-length skirt, took one step in. "There's someone to see you, Mr. Preston." She looked at him in puzzlement, obviously surprised by the way he was dressed. "Why are you . . . ? There's someone to see you."

"I need a few minutes, please."

"Yes, sir." She stepped out and closed the door.

It was almost certainly film noir. Presumably, he was a detective, and the person who wanted to see him was a client or potential client. Well, screw that. He got a kick out of watching those movies, sometimes, if Herbert Bradcock wasn't in them, and he liked the setting, but he didn't want to live through one of the plots. He didn't want to pry information from assholes, and he didn't want to be beaten up or threatened. He wouldn't mind stumbling across a body, in a fictional world, but it wouldn't be worth all the rest.

He looked at the trench coat. It was rumbled and well-worn. He liked trench coats, but he'd never owned one. He tried it on, and got the usual perfect fit. He walked back to the desk and looked to see if there was anything on it he wanted. There was a desk blotter, a large lighter, a box of cigars, miscellaneous papers, a phone book, a couple of other books. There was also the gun, of course, but he decided he wouldn't be needing it. He stopped looking—he wasn't on a treasure hunt. He wouldn't check out the drawers. He wasn't even sure if the money was the same here, but screw it. He moved toward the door. There was something heavy in a pocket of the coat. He took it out—a pint of whiskey, a brand he'd never heard of, "King Harry," the name in a kind of Merry Olde England script. It was about half full. He set it on the desk. He checked the other pockets. The only other thing he found was a skeleton key, not on a ring. He looked at it closely, then dropped it on the desk.

He walked out of the office. The adjoining room was also an office, a little smaller, but—unlike his—neatly kept. Across from him was another door with a pebble glass pane. This one said, backward, "GEORGE PRESTON, PRIVATE INVESTIGATOR." Sitting behind a desk, facing him, opening envelopes with a letter opener, was the woman he'd just spoken to. Sitting on a wooden chair beside the desk, also facing him, was another woman, pretty, early twenties, modest dress, rather large mouth. They looked up at him. Their expressions said he looked strange. The younger woman said, a little nervously, "Mr. Preston...."

The other woman, surprised but handling this in a businesslike manner, said, "You're ready, sir?"

George: "No. Uh... I think I'll quit the detective business. The place is yours. You can have whatever's in my apartment too. I think I'll leave town. Have a good life." To the younger woman he said: "I don't think I'm your man. Good luck with your problem."

The older woman looked annoyed. The younger woman, confused, said, "I... I see." He walked briskly out of the office.

The hall was narrow and barren. He followed it to a staircase with a wooden handrail and followed that down three floors to a small, drab lobby, from which he went out into the street. He turned left outside his building and followed the sidewalk. The handlers, he reflected, would not be surprised. The street looked better from down here. He liked the cars, though they were too similar to each other for his taste. A lot of them showed the outline of a spare tire in metal in the back—he liked the way that looked. The weather was cool but not unpleasant. He buttoned the trench coat.

People looked at him oddly—he didn't look right, wearing sneakers. Most of the men looked somewhere from late thirties to late fifties, though he saw one twenty-something guy in a leather jacket, without a hat. Even this guy wasn't wearing blue jeans. He saw more men than women. The women varied from early twenties to early fifties. They wore lighter colors than the men. He saw a few kids, all with adults, but, except for a few women, none of the adults had the youthful look that was so common in his own time. There were ornate street lamps and street signs, which looked quaint to him. The buildings also seemed quaint; the fronts looked decorous and, in some cases, almost stately. Few of the buildings were more than six stories tall. The tallest he saw was maybe a dozen stories. Occasionally he heard a honk in the distance. Occasionally a boxy police car or taxi rolled by. He guessed it was the '40s. He was enjoying the scenery; he felt good.

A car pulled over next to him, headed, of course, in the opposite direction. He heard Sullok's voice say, "George." He stopped and turned. Sullok was getting out. He'd parked quickly and sloppily, at an angle with the curb. The cars had to swerve a little to avoid him. Someone honked at him. Someone else yelled, "Yer blockin' the road, mac!" He ignored them. He wore a dark suit, a hat, and a striped tie. He took off the hat, and his ponytail spilled out. Looking at George, he asked, "Do you know where you're going?"

George shook his head and smiled. Sullok smiled and nodded. As George turned away, Sullok started to get back in the car. Walking, George heard the car door close, then he heard the car pull away.

He kept walking. There was some litter on the street, no broken glass. He met no one else who seemed to know him, which was fine. He wondered how long he'd have to walk to get to the outskirts of the city, and what lay beyond the city. So far the basic scenery hadn't changed much. He'd walked ten or so blocks, and everything still looked similar to what he'd seen where he started, by the detective office. He doubted, however, that he'd make it out of the city. He thought about Sullok. He wondered what motivated Sullok. Why did he play this game? What was he getting out of it? What had he done before George came along? What would he do after George? What did he think about? What did he want?

A wooden door in a frame appeared, with the usual "thump," on the sidewalk about ten yards in front of him. He kept his pace more or less the same. People stopped and looked. Cars slowed down. He heard people starting to talk in tones of wonderment. He stopped in front of the door, reached for the knob, turned it, and pulled the door open.

There was his apartment. He swallowed, then stepped through. Even as he did, he wondered if this was what he wanted.

Inside the apartment, he looked around—it looked the same. Again he made a point of not looking back quickly to see if the world doorway was still there. Outside it was dark. His bathroom door was open, and what he could see of it looked the way it always had, a towel on the towel rack and another on the floor by the tub, various items on the sink. He turned to look at the clock radio on the dresser. He would have seen the world doorway if it was still there, and it wasn't. The clock radio showed 8:07 p.m. He'd left in the afternoon, around 3:00. He went to his computer and tapped on the mouse. The screen came up—the time it showed was 8:06 p.m. He moved the pointer to that and got the date—January 21. He'd left the day before.

He looked in the next room at the note cards on his kitchen table, the book about Harper, and the glass of tea, in which the ice had long since melted. He looked out the window, though he couldn't see much. So he was back, and here was his life. He could do whatever he wanted. He could tell people about this, or write about it, or keep it to himself, or hint about it, or whatever he wanted. He felt relieved and sad. He felt unbelief but didn't doubt that it had happened. He wondered briefly how he ought to feel, then thought, screw that. It was his experience; he'd feel however he wanted.

He checked his pockets. He took out his wallet, a telegram, a pocket watch, a bandana, and a stack of twenties folded in half, and set it all on his dresser, where his keys were already sitting, among other things. Then he took off the trench coat and threw it on his bed. He changed clothes, even his sneakers, switching to an old pair he got from his closet. It crossed his mind to shave but he decided not to. He took a heavy jacket out of his closet and put it on. It had gloves and a hat in its pockets.

Would he ever find out why or how any of it had happened? He doubted it. He could live with that.

He grabbed his wallet and keys from his dresser, pocketed them, and walked to his apartment door. It wasn't locked. He opened it. There was Sullok. He was wearing blue jeans, a gray t-shirt, white sneakers, and the ponytail. They looked at each other across the doorway. Sullok said, "Hello."

"Hi."

"Do you mind if I come in?"

George didn't feel angry toward him, although he thought maybe he should. He said: "Yeah. Come in." He turned around and walked deeper into the room, and Sullok followed him. He turned again and motioned with his hand toward the armchair. "Have a seat."

"Thanks." Sullok sat down.

"Can I get you anything? Maybe a water? I don't have much." Should he be offering anything? Sullok had shot him, and he'd shot Sullok twice, not counting the computer game. Actually, that made it seem like he owed Sullok, and maybe he did, but of course there was more to it than that. He dropped the line of thought.

Sullok answered: "I'm fine. Thanks."

George went to the cushioned desk chair in front of his computer, swiveled it around to face Sullok, and sat down. He still had the jacket on. The apartment had come furnished, of course with old furniture. The desk chair was the one piece of furniture that George owned. The armchair Sullok was sitting in faced the television, in a corner—he turned it so he was facing George. George asked, "So . . . can you tell me what this is about?"

Sullok nodded. "Yes."

This threw George. In a way he had expected it—why else would Sullok be here? But it still felt unbelievable to him. After a while, he asked, "Was any of that real?"

"Yes and no. Not the way you mean."

"I wasn't dreaming."

"Of course not."

Something occurred to George that he hadn't thought of before, something scary. He made a sweeping motion with his hand. "Is this real?"

"It's the same. . . . Yes and no. Not the way you mean."

George nodded. It was too much to absorb. He looked around. The apartment was spare, but there were plenty of little things to see if you looked for them. On the carpet in front of the television there was a dark stain, maybe coffee, which had been there since before he moved in. Except it hadn't. "So . . . if none of this is real, what is real?"

Sullok thought for a few seconds. "It's not 2000. It's 2104. . . ."

George blurted out, "What—you've got a time machine?"

"No. They don't exist. We didn't bring you to the future. You've always been there. This is the past. . . . It's a simulation of the past. What they called it in 2000, the world you think you're a part of, was virtual reality. It's like a big game, but with no rules and no objectives. The places you went were all like that. There might be a scenario you could follow, but you could decide not to follow it. You could explore in the worlds, interact with the characters. And you did. We recorded all of it. You'll get a copy."

"Never mind the copy. And never mind the other worlds. I had . . . I remember a whole life here. . . . None of it happened?"

"Not the way you mean."

"How long have I been here?"

"Before you walked through the first doorway?"

"Right."

"A few hours. It all started when you woke up that morning. Everything before that never happened."

"Okay. . . . You messed with my memory."

"Yes. You agreed to it. . . ."

"So who am I really? Is George Preston even my name?"

"Yes. You're a lot like you think you are. . . ."

"I don't think anything anymore."

"You know what I mean. You're 27. You're a graduate student. You look like you do here, except for styles being different, of course. You live in Sawyerville; you're from Unionville. Your parents and your sister are a lot like your memory of them."

"And who are you? What's your name? Are you even a person?"

"Yes. My name is Walter Hamilton. I work for a company that lets people have virtual reality vacations. This is what I look like, mostly."

"So I'm really in a tube or something."

"Something like that. It's not a tube. You're lying on a bed being monitored. Think of a hospital room."

"And so are you?"

"Yes, in a different room. More than one person can plug into the same adventure."

"Was anybody else real? I mean, controlled by a real person?"

"No."

"Terry? Lacey?" He laughed, but it wasn't funny. He felt like a fool. "Pistol Kramer? They were all just . . . characters?"

Sullok, who was really Hamilton, said, "I'm sorry." George looked down and shook his head. Sullok/Hamilton continued: "We're not talking about simulations from 2000. A simulated person can fool people now."

That might be, George thought, but the characters he'd bonded with were, in large part, clichés. On the other hand, they had had emotions, or seemed to. And then he was worried about them again. "Were they sentient?"

"No. Not at all. They were just characters controlled by the game. When you leave a world, it shuts down, but nobody dies."

George took a deep breath. He didn't know what to say. He shook his head. "That scared me."

"I know. But don't worry about that. No one got hurt."

They were both quiet for a while. Then George said, "Sorry I killed you. Or tried to. Twice."

"It's alright. I killed you first."

"That's true. . . . But you knew it wasn't real."

"Did you think it was real?"

"I don't know. . . . No, I didn't think I was killing you. And the second time I knew I wasn't."

"Alright then." Hamilton got out of the chair, walked over to George, and offered George his hand. George hesitated—they hadn't settled everything. But he shook anyway. Hamilton smiled and then returned to the armchair.

George asked: "So what's the world like? The real world?"

"It's good enough that there's at least one business offering people virtual reality vacations."

That annoyed George. "No kidding. What else?"

"Actually, I'm not going to get into that. The world's fine. When this is all over your memory will come back, along with your understanding of the world you live in. It'd be jarring to get it all now. You know you're from 2104, but your memories are still from 2000. And those memories we planted will fade away. Not your memories of playing the game, of course—those are real."

"Okay." As far as what Hamilton was saying about his planted memories and his real memories, he got it, and he didn't want to talk about it. As far as finding out what the world was like, he wasn't going to argue. Hamilton wouldn't talk, and if Hamilton was telling him it wouldn't be good for him to find out now, it probably wouldn't be. And he didn't feel that curious about it right now. It felt alien, even though he knew it was the world he actually lived in. Changing the subject, he asked: "Why don't you let people know the places they go aren't real? Aren't you scaring the hell out of them?"

"They do know the places aren't real. And most people don't go to multiple places. What you went through was special. I shot you dead in the first adventure so you'd know you were safe after that."

"Actually, I wasn't sure."

"I'm sorry about that. You acted like you thought you were safe."

George sighed. "I mostly did think that. But there's thinking something and there's knowing something. . . . Never mind. I'm not mad about it. Not right now. So what was special about my . . . adventure?"

"Like I said, you didn't know it wasn't real."

"No, I mean, why didn't you let me know? And why send me to multiple worlds? Why do it differently with me? And what's with going back to 2000? Why do that? Actually, why not just . . . if you didn't want me to know, for whatever reason, why not just have me in a simulation of my real life and have the door pop up? And what if I didn't go through?" He stopped. He couldn't help smiling.

Hamilton seemed to be wondering where to start. Then he said: "We'd have offered you other doorways. Eventually, if you never stepped through one, we'd just have you wake up in another world. Simulating your real life wouldn't have worked. You can't get every detail of someone's actual life right. You wouldn't have believed it. But we could've gotten around that. You could've just woken up in an adventure. You wouldn't have thought you were dreaming—the adventures are nothing like anyone's dreams. They look real, and they feel real. The problem is that someone who knows he's from 2104 would immediately suspect the new world was virtual reality. We had to go back to a time when virtual reality was much more primitive."

"Okay. So why keep me in the dark in the first place? What was the point? And why me? What's special about me?"

"You were a graduate student writing a dissertation on Paul Harper. You are, I mean. Your field is 20$^{th}$ Century American Literature. And you like books, movies, et cetera from the 20$^{th}$ Century. Think of a guy in 2000 who likes Edwin Hobson mysteries, and other things from that era. You were perfect for us. I found out about you from my cousin. He knows you from grad school. And why we wanted to do it in the first place . . . . It was an experiment. We wanted to see what happened, how you reacted."

"You want to have people pay to go on adventures without knowing they're not real? You'll scare people. You won't get many takers."

"But we'd get some. It'd be scary, but it'd be exciting."

"And how many people are big 20$^{th}$ Century literature buffs?"

"Not enough for a market. You're right. But we could work on that. Spend more on altering people's memories, and get better at it. And you didn't *have* to be a 20$^{th}$ Century guy—that just helped. . . . We could put someone in a 20$^{th}$ Century detective movie who had never seen one; he could still enjoy it. But like I said, it was an experiment. It wasn't a trial run, like you're thinking. We're not going to start doing this next year. There's an excellent chance we never will. It was an experiment. We wanted to see what would happen. It didn't necessarily have to lead to anything."

"You spent all that money and time . . . ."

"It didn't cost as much as you think. And people aren't as money-conscious as they were in 2000. It wasn't about money. You didn't do it for money—you didn't make any money. I spent more time on it than anybody, including you. Not that I'm saying you can compare that to actually going through it . . . . But, anyway . . . I'm paid by the company, but I didn't do it for money. It was something I wanted to do. Almost like we were making art. . . . Did Harper write just for the money?"

"Harper was a jerk."

"I know he was a jerk. That's not the point. I'm asking—did he write just for the money?"

"No. He didn't." George thought some more. "Alright, I actually felt things. I mean, physically. I ran and got tired, I was wounded. I got stabbed in the back with a sword. . . ."

Hamilton nodded. "Right. By stimulating the right parts of your brain we could make you feel all that. Eating, drinking, going to the bathroom, having sex, being punched. Your body didn't experience any of it. Computers controlled it, with human oversight. . . . The record of the game is just sights and sounds, of course, from your point of view."

George thought about it. The brain-stimulating business was creepy, but how else could they do it? What else did he want to know? He seemed to have asked about all the important things. "Okay. What about the sleeping? Why did I want to sleep so much?"

"It's part of the experience. It's draining. We can also increase that effect, and we do. It helps us manage the whole thing."

He hadn't asked all the important things. "And why send me where you sent me? Who picked the worlds?"

"Well, you picked two of them while you were in the game. And we gave you doorways you could decide to go through, or not. You and I talked about where you'd go beforehand, and I worked with other people in the company. You didn't get to go wherever you wanted, and you agreed to that. The final decision on each world was mine."

George shook his head. "You were 'the handlers' all along. I imagined some kind of committee. I thought you were the one guy who wasn't in on it."

"Well, you didn't think you were in on it either, but you were. . . . I was on your side. As far as I'm concerned."

George didn't say anything for a few seconds, then he said, "Thanks." He was quiet again, thinking. Then he asked, "So what if I hadn't come back through that last door?"

"Kind of like if you hadn't entered. We would've offered it to you again. Eventually, if you never accepted, you'd just wake up in reality, in 2104. You made it clear you wanted to come back, or we wouldn't have offered it so soon. We would have let you stay in another day or so."

"That's okay." He didn't regret coming back when he did. He thought about what he'd done in the game. "I spent the whole time complaining. . . ."

Hamilton cut him off. "No, you didn't. You did a lot of things, and you had a lot of fun. You fought that giant, from the air. You got together with Terry. We had that fight in the John Thorpe world. . . . I'll grant you, you did do some complaining."

"And I was pissed off at whoever was doing it. I was the one doing it. Not exactly, but I agreed to everything."

"I think a lot of people would've been angry. You did a lot of things."

George hadn't just complained. He'd done things. Hamilton had mentioned some good things. He'd also gone on the adventure with Pistol Kramer. He'd walked through the film noir city. He'd done a lot of things. He couldn't have known beforehand how he'd react. He asked, "So what happens now?"

"Go to sleep whenever you're ready. You'll wake up in the real world. We'll debrief you. I'll be there."

"Okay." He shook his head. "So I've got another few hours in 2000."

"If you want them."

George stood up, and smiled. He still had the heavy jacket on. "I'll take 'em. I think I'll go for a walk. I was going to go to the coffee house, but, enough characters. . . . You're welcome to come with. Probably won't be too exciting though."

"I'll pass. See you later."

"Okay." George walked over and shook the man's hand again. Then he turned and left the apartment, and went for a long walk.

# ABOUT THE AUTHOR

Brian Deason lives in Collinsville, Illinois, a suburb of St. Louis, Missouri, with his wife Tara Perry and their children, Conal and Nora. In 2001 he received a Ph.D. degree from Southern Illinois University at Carbondale. He has been a small-town newspaper reporter and a community college teacher, and is now a civil servant. This is his first novel.

Made in the USA
San Bernardino, CA
12 July 2016